JUMMY AT THE
RIVER SCHOOL

A MESSAGE FROM CHICKEN HOUSE

I wish I'd gone to a boarding school as fun as this one! It's fantastic: there are wild animals, midnight feasts, friendships and rivalries. But as well as a rousing adventure, wonderful debut author Sabine Adeyinka has written a serious story with high stakes – poverty and lack of opportunity cause real danger to characters we grow to love. Luckily we have the resourceful Jummy to put things right in the end – she's a blast! More please, Sabine – back next term?

BARRY CUNNINGHAM
Publisher
Chicken House

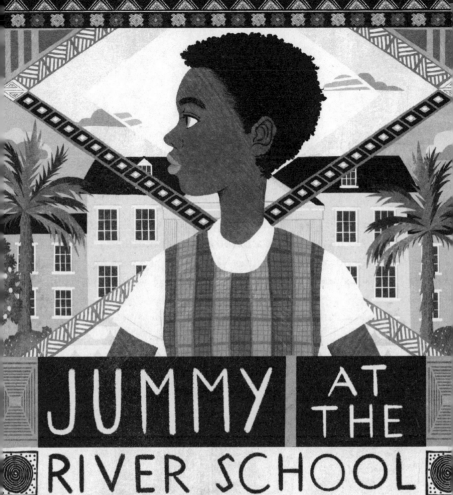

JUMMY AT THE
RIVER SCHOOL

SABINE
ADEYINKA

Chicken
House

2 Palmer Street, Frome,
Somerset BA11 1DS
www.chickenhousebooks.com

Text © Sabine Adeyinka 2022
Illustration © Hanako Clulow 2022

First published in Great Britain in 2022
Chicken House
2 Palmer Street
Frome, Somerset BA11 1DS
United Kingdom
www.chickenhousebooks.com

Chicken House/Scholastic Ireland, 89E Lagan Road, Dublin Industrial Estate,
Glasnevin, Dublin D11 HP5F, Republic of Ireland

Cover and interior design by Helen Crawford-White
Typeset by Dorchester Typesetting Group Ltd
Printed and bound in Great Britain by CPI Group (UK) Ltd, Croydon CR0 4YY

FSC
www.fsc.org
MIX
Paper from
responsible sources
FSC® C020471

1 3 5 7 9 10 8 6 4 2

British Library Cataloguing in Publication data available.

PB ISBN 978-1-913696-04-7
eISBN 978-1-913696-27-6

*For Ayo, Shindara and Seni; for believing
and therefore, understanding.*

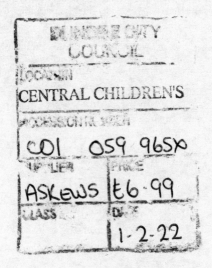

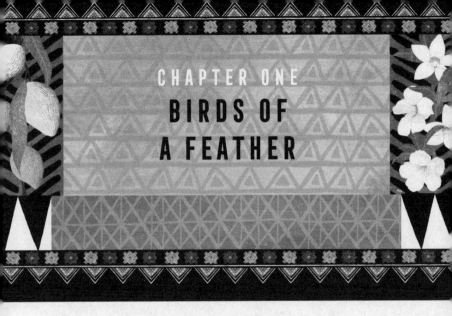

CHAPTER ONE
BIRDS OF
A FEATHER

I woke up startled by the shriek of the cockerel from the backyard.

Someone must have disturbed it. It was the laziest cockerel you could ever meet.

A tiny pebble hit one of the windowpanes.

I dragged myself from my bed, my khaki uniform crumpled from my afternoon nap, and got to my bedroom window just in time to see Owolabi's large frame disappear from view. He must have disturbed the cockerel again because it shrieked even more fearfully than before.

I rolled my eyes. Owolabi lived in the flat above mine and was the most annoying boy – no,

1

scratch that – *person* I had ever met. I was sure Caro's cockerel agreed with me.

Caro! That was when I remembered my problem. I needed to find my best friend fast. She would help me out of this trouble I was in.

I shuffled into my brown school shoes, stepping on the backs as usual, and peeped through the bead curtains that separated our bedrooms from the living room. Mummy was seated at the dining table, picking rice. First, she smoothed the rice over on the tray with the back of her hand, then she picked out the undesirable grains and put them into a tiny bowl. She was humming that tune that meant she was a million miles away.

I crept past the dining room and into the kitchen. Made it!

'Hey, Jumoke!'

I jumped out of my skin.

'Why haven't you changed or eaten since you came back from school, ehn, why?'

Joy, Mummy's helper, was in the kitchen and was judging the ink marks on my uniform with her disapproving side-eye as she picked the beans that would go with the rice.

'I cannot eat and I cannot even think about changing my clothes.' I held out my hands towards her. 'I am in hot soup!'

'This girl, for someone so small, you get into a lot of trouble. What have you done this time?'

'Nothing!' I snapped, and left our flat at top speed. The mosquito-net door shook with just the right amount of gusto.

'For someone so small, my foot! What does my size have to do with anything?' I muttered angrily to myself. I had been going to tell Joy about my predicament, but not any more! I was so fed up of being treated like a small girl at home. When were they going to realize that I was eleven already and no longer a baby? Besides, Joy was not in my school: how would she know if other people got into trouble more than me?

I could not wait to get to boarding school. I tried to picture myself in the illustrious River School, the best secondary school for girls in Southern Nigeria. I had taken the entry exams and everyone who knew us was waiting to see if I would make it in. Baba and Mummy would be so proud if I did. I had worked hard for the first time in my life but I wasn't sure I had done enough. I imagined myself in my River School dress doing stuff by myself. I would make my own way with no one trying to help me all the time. I thought of midnight feasts, giggling late into the night in the dorms, noisy meals in the big dining hall and, best of all, games and picnics by the river. The results would be out any time now and I was on edge with anticipation.

Owolabi had already received his results. The whole neighbourhood knew he was going to Kingswill College, the boys' school near the River School. He had run out of his flat with the admission letter in his hands, shouting, 'I passed! I passed!' Joy and I had rushed out on to the balcony to see him carrying Caro's brother in the air in celebration. Later they were found sitting in the large dustbin in front of our block of flats drinking soda. Those boys were so strange.

I could not wait to be rid of primary school with all its silly problems.

For today's particular task, we had been told to finish drawing a map of Nigeria during our short break before the teacher came into class. I was not very good at drawing but that wasn't even what irritated me. It was one more day till the end of primary school, so the teacher was just being wicked. We should have been playing cards, skipping or doing backflips at the back of the classroom.

I was just about to carry on with my weak attempt at the map when I saw the hungry look in Chigozie's eyes as I slid the juicy mango slices that Joy had prepared for me down my throat. Chigozie was the class captain and good at drawing. He sat across from me.

'Do you want mango, Chigozie?' I stared deeply into his hungry eyes.

He nodded vigorously.

'Do you know how to draw the map of Nigeria?'

He nodded even harder.

I stretched out my hand with the bowl of mango in it, and he appeared beside me in a flash. I left my geography book open and went out to play. But the teacher caught him doing my work and gave me lines, one hundred of them.

So that's why I needed to find Caro. She would help me write my lines!

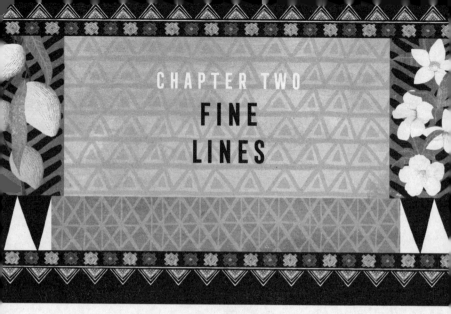

CHAPTER TWO

FINE LINES

I found Caro plucking fruit from the tree in front of the staff quarters, which housed all the workers like Joy who serviced our flats. Caro, her six siblings and parents lived in just two bedrooms. I had never been into her place and she had never been into mine. In front of the fruit tree, though, was common ground.

I could never understand why fruit didn't come with its own name like the pineapple or pawpaw. Everybody just called it 'fruit' and plucked it from the tree in school as if it showed you had some form of strength. It was not juicy like mango where you could chase its juice with your tongue all the way down your arm, even if you were in public. Fruit was just dry red flesh and I hated it.

Baba said the nut inside was called an almond. He had crushed fruit with a stone one day on the balcony to expose a flat brown nut. He gave it to me to taste and I spat it out. I could feel its gritty bits clinging to my gums. I was not impressed. I had never seen anyone selling fruit in any kind of market. It was simply on its tree for you to pluck. A very bulky and untidy tree, normally blocking the view of something far more important.

Don't ever confuse fruit with other fruits. They are not the same thing!

'Caro, come and help me,' I called up to her. 'They have given me a hundred lines to write in school and I have to do it by tomorrow.'

'Wait, let me just pluck this one,' she shouted down to me. 'Chei! This one will sweet well well.'

She climbed down from the tree chewing the fruit like an old man. She spat it on the floor and bit into it again as if she were eating sugar cane.

Her long hair was in its usual four squares of threaded plaits and her big brown eyes were the same rich colour as her skin. We were the same age but she towered over me in a rather regal sort of way.

'So what did they give you to write this time? This girl, every day, you de enter trouble!'

Caro could speak really well when she wanted to, but she was always switching between proper and pidgin English once she was relaxed. At school, if you spoke pidgin, you had to pay ten kobo to the English teacher. And ten kobo could buy five sweets.

I shrugged. 'I will never give anyone my homework to do on my behalf again.'

She looked at me incredulously and we both burst into laughter.

'Spare me the lecture,' I said. 'Are you going to help me?'

Caro grinned. 'No problem, I can finish it in one hour. Wetin you go gi'me?' Her eyes were wide with hope.

'I will get you something from upstairs, don't worry.'

'I want five big agbalumo!'

There was only one thing Caro loved more than fruit and that was agbalumo. I had to agree with her on this one. Agbalumo is the fruit that Eve must have taken from the snake. It is the most beautiful of fruits. You can rub it between your palms for a long time like a ball until it gets soft. Then, you pierce a hole through it with your teeth and draw out the sweet pink sap, praying and hoping you are not eating a maggot at the same time. Then you open it and suck on the four or five seeds covered in pink flesh and more sweet sap until they reveal the shiniest chocolate-brown seeds you ever saw. When they are dried, you can use them as counters to solve world-changing arithmetics. Finally, you eat the sweet, succulent pink flesh and chew the skin just like chewing gum. Agbalumo is a big deal.

'Ehn, five? Are you mad? Where will I get five from? Besides, you can't finish in one hour.'

'I can! I will use three pens joined together with elastic, I just did one for ThankGod.'

ThankGod was the youngest of Caro's big brothers and Owolabi's best friend.

'OK, OK, meet me at the back stairs as soon as they start the seven o'clock news and try not to pour palm oil on the lines this time.'

Caro stuck out her tongue at me and picked up a large metal bucket at the bottom of the fruit tree. I followed her towards the outside tap.

'Are you going to play ride over, ride over with us today?' I asked. This was our favourite game in the compound – there were two teams, one linking hands and the other trying to break through.

'Ah, I can't o. I have to fetch water for my family and now you have given me this big work to finish by seven.'

'You have to play!' I said. 'Tomorrow is the last day of school and everyone will go away to their villages for summer.' I wasn't even sure we were going to Ekiti this summer but I was desperate.

Caro was ride over, ride over champion. If she didn't play, we would really struggle. With Caro on our team, we always won.

Even the day the other team demanded we hand over Owolabi, we still won. They had chosen him because he was the biggest, but he was in no way the tallest or the strongest. That title belonged to Caro! All we had to do was wait until they called Caro's number: 'Ride over, ride over, we call number four to ride over.' The fear in their faces as they realized with horror that Caro was number four! She raced fiercely towards them, and went straight for Owolabi who was linked with a much smaller boy. She raised her hands to break through their link and the smaller boy yanked his hand away in fear. His teammates groaned as Caro took Owolabi captive and brought him back over to our team.

We cheered and chanted several times:

You no fit beat Caro! A ye ye Caro!
You no fit beat Caro! A ye ye Caro!

She did her usual victory dance, and whenever Caro danced, the celebration would last that bit longer. She would bend this way and that, her shoulders and back shaking gracefully, inviting everyone to join in. Even the opposition could not resist such an invitation.

'Jumoke, I can't play today,' Caro insisted now. 'I have to fill our water tank to the brim and it's only halfway.'

I knew that was a big task. We always had running water in our flat but Caro's family had to fetch water from the outside tap to use for cooking and bathing. They shared the kitchen and bathrooms with the other residents of the staff quarters.

I was still standing there scratching my head, wondering how my friend could play with us today, when all the children from the flats and staff quarters started coming out to play. Owolabi came from the staff quarters with ThankGod, his Polaroid camera swinging this way and that as he gesticulated and laughed loudly.

There was something about the way all the children approached, moving in a straight line towards me . . . Suddenly, I could see what I needed to do. I looked at the rushing tap, at the metal bucket and at Caro.

'That's it!' I shouted. 'I can help you fetch the water.'

'You, this tiny thing, you can't even carry half a bucket of water.'

'I don't have to be able to carry it far. Everyone! Stop where you are!'

Everyone stopped and looked at me. Owolabi and ThankGod eyed me coolly and I could see they were about to protest.

'If Caro doesn't finish fetching water, she can't play,' I informed them.

Owolabi's eyes flashed wide. 'OK. We're listening.'

'Caro,' I said. 'Pass me that bucket of water and get a few more empty ones from inside.'

I lifted the bucket of water. It was so heavy. Owolabi grinned and nudged ThankGod. I couldn't let him see me fail. His hands were already poised to snap any evidence with his Polaroid. I grew magic muscles and passed the bucket of water to the person nearest to me, pointing in the direction of Caro's water tank.

Everyone got it at once. Each person passed the bucket to the next until it reached the end of the line where Caro was now waiting to pour the water in. I ran quickly to her to return the empty bucket to the tap. Caro smiled at me.

'Jummy! You this small girl with big sense!' she said, then shouted to the others, 'Stop wasting the water. Careful, it's spilling everywhere.'

We were at it for half an hour when Caro cried out, 'The tank don full!'

We all cheered loudly.

I was the only person still in school uniform and it was soaking wet but I didn't care. We were going to play ride over, ride over and we were going to win!

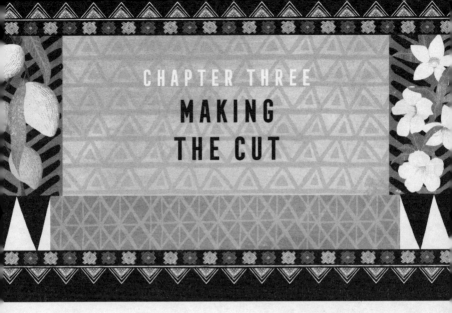

CHAPTER THREE

MAKING THE CUT

'Jumoke!'

It was my mother's voice. I pictured her leaning over the balcony looking left and right, impatiently. I must be in hot soup because she had not sent Joy to fetch me.

'Jumoke!'

This time it was a shriek. Maybe Joy had told Mummy that I slammed the door on her earlier. Or perhaps she'd found out about the drawing or the lines. I racked my brain trying to remember what else I could have done.

I raced up the back stairs like a gazelle, ignoring loads of steps on the way. I could hear the noise of the other children still rattling below. Our ride over, ride over team had regrouped and were now having a water fight. I ran past the pungent smell of periwinkles and vegetable soup on the first floor and made my way to face my fate. I swung the kitchen door open and walked into a room full of adults: Baba and Mummy; Auntie Heather, our Ghanaian neighbour, resident baker and seamstress; Owolabi's mum from the flat upstairs; and Uncle Yombo, Baba's youngest brother. This gathering would not have been strange if it had been a weekend.

Joy was scrambling around the room with various fizzy drinks, tumblers, ice cubes, chinchin and cashew nuts served on our best saucers. I hoped it was Auntie Heather's home-made chinchin. They were full of sugar and always freshly fried when she brought them down. They were crunchy on the outside and soft on the inside because she put in so much butter.

'Pop!' went the fizzy drinks as they were opened, but it did not go with the look on everyone's faces. They all looked so serious. I stood behind one of the chairs, trying to hide my wet uniform.

'Jumoke, read this.' Baba handed me a letter.

My heart froze. Perhaps my class teacher had written to my parents about me giving my work to others. I opened the letter with trembling hands. My eyes were darting across the words, refusing to focus. I squinted and took a deep breath. It was from the River School.

> It gives me great pleasure to inform you that Jumoke has been offered a place at the River School. She performed most impressively in our entrance tests, so please pass on my congratulations to her . . .

My face broke into the widest smile and all the adults started smiling too. Nobody cared about my wet dress. This was a celebration, not a scolding!

I had been accepted into the River School!

There was a loud cheer from everyone. Owolabi's mummy squeezed twenty naira into my hands. 'You will love it,' she said. 'You remember Owolabi's cousin Lola who visited last year? She is in Form Two now at the River School and will take care of you.'

I remembered Lola and liked her a lot. She had a bright face that shone like the sun. She was always full of funny stories from boarding school and had a shrieking laugh that brought everyone to fits. Her stories about the River School had made me study harder for the exams. I, too, wanted to sit eating sticky snacks with my friends and watching the river flow by.

Baba looked at me and then at Mummy. 'Your mother and I are very proud of you.'

Auntie Heather laughed. 'Why didn't you send your baby far away like some other people?'

Mummy pulled me towards her and lifted up my arm. 'This one is my only child o! See her tiny arm like stegomyia mosquito.' Everyone laughed.

'I'm like you, Mummy, tiny but mighty!' I lifted my arm and flexed its muscles. Baba let out his wild cackle. It sounded like a cat scratching on a metal water tank.

He was still laughing when he pointed the remote control towards the TV and the volume came up. The drums and chimes sprang forth, signalling the start of the seven o'clock news. Everyone sat up in their seats. Those chimes were to adults like the sound of an ice-cream van to children and I knew it would no longer be about me. Anyway, Caro would have finished the lines by now.

'Mummy, can I take agbalumo?'

She waved her hand in approval, and dismissal.

I left the room, grabbed only three agbalumos from the fruit bowl on the kitchen counter, and ran back down the dimly lit back stairs.

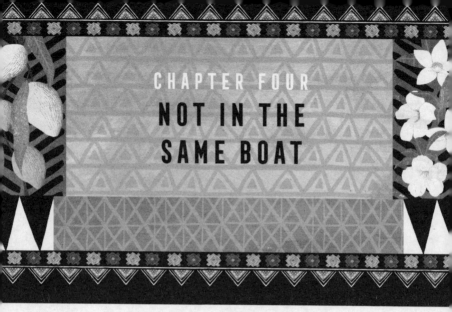

aro's father had built a small wooden canopy outside their bedroom window to sell cooked food and cold drinks to the workers in the area. I couldn't see Caro's face clearly but I could see her four threaded plaits standing up in the light. She looked just like the newscasters with only her head and shoulders emerging from the window. Light music played from the small radio to her left and there was a lantern to her right. There were several men sitting on the three benches under the canopy eating and chatting quietly. I waited for Caro to finish serving one of the drivers.

'Your money no complete just like every day

this month,' Caro said quietly but firmly.

'I will give you tomorrow,' the man replied. 'How much do I owe you?'

'Forty-eight naira and thirty-six kobo,' Caro announced.

The driver shook his head and laughed. 'See this small girl, she get money sense o!' The other men laughed too.

'Tomorrow I will not serve you food o!' Caro smiled and handed him a steaming plate of rice.

'Ahem!' I coughed to get her attention. She nodded at me.

'ThankGod, come and sell o,' she called, and disappeared from the window.

ThankGod's head was now in the window and I could hear Caro reeling off instructions. He quickly started to write them on the notepad by the window.

'Make sure you collect their money for the food. Samson 2.50, Nteko 4.30, Bitrus 2.60 and Driver, same story.' ThankGod and Caro chuckled knowingly.

'Dis girl, you are still in your uniform,' said Caro when she came out. 'And where is my agbalumo?' She tapped gently on the brown envelope tucked into her wrapper. I too tapped on my side pockets and grinned at her. We made our way towards the bottom of the back stairs, the cool evening air embracing us.

I reached into my pockets and gave her three agbalumos.

'Here! I will give you the remaining later,' I said. 'Anything I ask for now, they will give me. I just passed my exams to go to the River School!'

Caro did not say anything. She just took the agbalumo solemnly and stared back at me.

'Didn't you hear what I said? I passed! I am going to boarding school!'

'Yes, yes, I heard what you said.'

'Then what is the matter with you? Why are you looking like that?'

She avoided my eyes. If I didn't know better I would have thought she was about to cry. She retied her wrapper and plunked herself at the bottom of the stairs.

'Who will I play with now?'

My heart skipped a beat. I had been so caught up in the excitement of the River School, I didn't think about Caro being alone. Between her chores and running the kiosk, she would have no time to make new friends. Caro was good at everything from numbers to dancing to plucking fruit.

'But you said you didn't want to go.'

'Yes, that was before.' Her voice began to shake.

I sat down beside her. 'There are some schools that you don't need exams to enter.'

'You don't understand.' She shook her head. 'Nobody imagines me going to secondary school. All my siblings have stopped at primary school so why should I be different?'

'Maybe because you didn't tell them you want to go to school. If you just—'

'You can't understand, Jummy. You don't have any responsibilities. Your parents can help you with everything. I have to help my parents.'

'My parents didn't help me pass my exams, I studied very hard,' I snapped back at once.

'Yes, but everyone in your house wants you to go to the River School. Nothing is in your way.'

'Who told you? Before today, everyone thought I was too tiny to go to boarding school. They didn't even think I could pass the exams. Some of the neighbours said I will not make it past a term in boarding school. Well, I will show them!'

'Well, I am not you. Sometimes you just have to do things because of your family. But I cannot ask you to understand that!'

'But Caro, there must be something you can—'

'O Jummy, just leave it, you can't really understand it. I'll be OK.'

Caro tried to give me her biggest smile. She was very good at flashing big smiles even when nothing was going her way.

She got up intently, pulled the envelope from inside her wrapper and handed it to me.

I opened it, still looking at her. She was defiant and I knew I had to let it go. I looked down at the paper in front of me. She had written all the lines.

I remembered I had some money in my pocket. I put five naira into Caro's hand just like Owolabi's mummy had just done with me. I felt all grown-up.

Caro kissed her teeth in shock. 'You want make my mama wound me dis night? I can't take money. Give me my two remaining agbalumo by weekend or else!'

Of course, she was right. My mother would kill me too if I suddenly appeared with unexplained money.

I tucked the envelope under my arm. 'I will get you a hundred agbalumo if you like.'

'Oya! Swear to me that you will write to me.'

I put my forefinger on my tongue and raised it to the sky. She did the same. We linked our pinky fingers together and laughed softly.

The night was bursting with stars. The music from the kiosk played in the distance.

'When you are not here, I will come outside and remember you.' Caro's voice was shaking again.

I nodded. I could not get any words out.

'Goodnight, Jummy.' Her voice was stronger now.

'Goodnight, Caro!' Mine was a whisper.

She turned towards the staff quarters and I stood there watching her walk away, her four plaits disappearing into the darkness.

CHAPTER FIVE

THE JOURNEY BEGINS

The summer went by really quickly. One minute I was climbing the water tank in Ekiti village square and the next I was sitting in the car on the way to the coach station.

Caro was nowhere to be seen for the entire summer. When we came back from Ekiti, her sister said she had gone to stay with Big Auntie and that she didn't know when she would be back. I gave her sister my River School address and hoped with all my heart that she would write. It felt so good jotting it down.

The River School

Private Mail Box 100
Ogun State, Nigeria

'Jumoke, we're almost there,' said Baba after we'd been driving for twenty minutes. 'The station is just on the right, can you see all those green coaches?' He wound down the window and pointed. The heat of the Lagos sun came in with full force and I could hear the loud horns and shouts of street hawkers selling their wares.

'Ice water tutu re!' a woman with a bucket on her head was crying out.

My heart started to skip several beats. I didn't know what to expect. I had dreamt all my life about going to boarding school but now it was here, I wasn't so sure.

Our car pulled into the coach station and there was a man with a Kingswill College cap directing us to the right. I saw several of the school's coaches in the opposite direction. I stretched my neck to see if I could see Owolabi, but all I saw was a sea of boys in brown khakis and white shirts.

'Look at all your schoolmates, Jumoke.'

Mummy was as excited as Baba.

There were several wooden sheds with long queues in front of them. There were girls in different-coloured checked dresses walking, running and skipping. I looked down proudly at my orange-checked pinafore dress. Auntie Heather had sewn it perfectly. It fitted nicely around the smart white short-sleeved blouse under it. You were allowed to make your pinafores in any style you liked as long as it wasn't tight or above the knee. Mine had a waist-band and two large pockets in front. I was thrilled to be in Nile House with Lola, Owolabi's cousin. She had told me that the six houses were named after some of the great African rivers: Nile, Niger, Senegal, Congo, Zambezi and Limpopo. I was also glad Nile House was orange; it didn't seem as ordinary as red or green.

Two girls passed by giggling. One of them shouted 'JJC' at me and I made a mental note to ask Lola what that meant.

'Come on, Jumoke,' Baba said, 'let's look for the housemistress, Mrs Aliu.'

He brought my black hard-shelled suitcase out

of the boot, and Mummy carried my travelling bag that held all the things I needed for tonight so that I wouldn't have to start rummaging through all my belongings. I carried my orange plastic bucket with my broom, cutlass and hoe poking out of the top. I could not for the life of me imagine using these tools. I had seen Caro and her family using them when tending to their small corn patch at the back of the staff quarters. At harvest, Caro's family roasted corn on a barbecue under the fruit tree and sold it with roasted groundnuts.

The keys to my suitcase and padlocks were jingling as I walked. Mummy had given me a key holder that I could wear like a belt. It coiled like our telephone cord at home and it was orange like my housewear.

We found the housemistress sitting at the shed furthest away, surrounded by girls in orange check waiting to be signed in. There was a suitcase opened in front of her and she was poking through it intently.

Mrs Aliu looked up. I liked her instantly. She was short and round and had a kind face, but I had a feeling she should not be messed with.

'Good afternoon, sir, good afternoon, Ma,' she said in a high-pitched voice that seemed to echo through my whole body. 'I am Mrs Aliu. I am your daughter's housemistress. Is she in Form One? What's her name?'

'Oya, Jumoke, speak up.' Baba gave me a nudge.

'Good afternoon, Ma.' I did the customary curtsey. 'My name is Jumoke Afolabi.'

She scrolled down her long sheet and smiled when she found my name.

'I hope you didn't bring contraband o,' she said, narrowing her eyes. 'We know all the tricks, we even check inside pillowcases!'

Baba let out his wild cackle of a laugh. 'No contraband here at all, we are a law-abiding family.'

Mrs Aliu chuckled too. 'Welcome to the River School, Jumoke. I am sure you will be a good girl. Go to that senior girl. She is Senior Moradeke. She is your Nile House captain.'

Senior Moradeke was tall and much bigger than Mrs Aliu. Her orange-checked skirt and blouse looked like they had been starched and pressed. She looked fierce. Mummy must have seen my apprehension.

'Come on, Jummy, let's go.'

When we got to Senior Moradeke, someone came behind me and covered my eyes with their hands.

I didn't know if I could laugh or play in front of my house captain.

'Who is this, please?' I said primly.

'Uh, who are you posing for?' came the reply.

Senior Moradeke butted in. 'Lola Fernando, before I open my eyes disappear from here.' She closed her eyes for a second and smiled.

I turned and saw it was Lola. She was giggling, her bright moon-shaped face reddening as she did so. She had her hair cut into a box style. It never occurred to me that I could do that.

'Good afternoon, Ma.' Senior Moradeke knelt on the concrete ground.

'Good afternoon, my dear.' My mother was beaming. Senior Moradeke had won her heart for life with her respectful greeting.

'You are in coach three.' Senior Moradeke gave me a set of handouts. One of them had the menu for the dining hall and another had maps of the school.

'There are a hundred and twenty-five girls in each house and you are in room one. Lola can show you around when we arrive but your name will be on your door. You will call those in Form Five "Senior" but you must show respect to even the girls only a year ahead of you. Three hundred and sixty-five days is not a joke!'

'You hear, Jummy?' Lola added. 'You must show respect to me.'

I wanted to box her ears. I didn't think I could remember any of the information Senior Moradeke had given me.

Baba carried my suitcase and bucket to the coach. He gave Lola five naira and me an envelope, and told me he had given Mrs Aliu some pocket money for me if I ran out of cash.

Mummy said a small prayer over me. 'Remember whose daughter you are,' she said. Then she put something into the travelling bag on my shoulder and winked at me.

'Jumoke will do us proud, just like Lola.' Baba gave Lola a high five and Mummy hugged me really tight.

'OK, Mummy, let me get on to the coach!'

'Be good!' That was Baba's customary way of saying goodbye but I think this time it was an order.

Lola and I walked to the coach. I wanted to look back but I was afraid because of the lump that was wedging itself in my throat. I didn't want to cry!

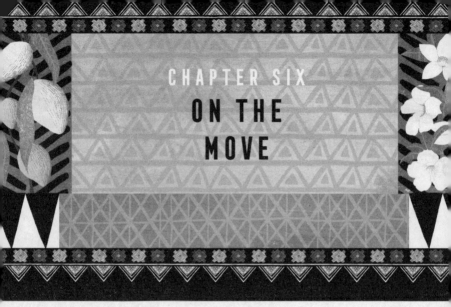

CHAPTER SIX
ON THE MOVE

There were a few Kingswill College boys talking to some senior girls outside the Nile House coach. Some of the boys looked even taller than Baba. Lola led the way on board and down the aisle to the middle. The coach was only half full but all the back seats were taken. The noise was tremendous.

'This doesn't look like it can take a hundred and twenty-five girls,' I said loudly, trying to be heard over the chatter.

'Oh, of course. This is just the coach from Lagos, there are others from all over the country,' Lola yelled back. 'Are you an aisle girl or window girl?'

34

'Window, please.' Even though it was a forty-five-minute ride, I wanted to daydream while staring out of the window.

'Good, I am an aisle girl. Aisle is where the action is.'

'Lola Fernando! Why didn't you phone me during the summer, see your big head!' a girl shouted as she made her way between the seats behind us. She had an interesting accent – Owolabi would have said it was 'Naijamerican'. I wondered whether he was on one of the Kingswill coaches already.

'Shut up, Gemini!' Lola retorted with a big grin.

Gemini's dress had giant squares instead of the regular tiny ones and was rather more agbalumo than the orange the rest of us were wearing. Her hair had loose curls and so her plaits refused to stay in place, though you could tell that someone had tried in vain to tame them. Most girls had really elaborate and neat cornrows or plaits, which looked as if they would last them about a month before they had to look for a friend to redo them. Mummy had cut mine short so I didn't have

35

to worry about that. I liked it but Owolabi had made fun of me. I was so glad there were no boys at the River School. They are so stupid!

'Who's the JJC?' Gemini jingled her keys at me.

'Go on, JJC, tell her who you are.' Lola's voice was full of fondness. 'Don't be afraid of her, she is only in Form Two, though she looks like she's fifteen.'

'Idiot!' Gemini cuffed Lola's head and grinned.

Someone at the back shouted, 'Senior Gemini, will you be my school mother?'

There was a roar of laughter.

'So what's the name?'

'Jumoke Afolabi,' I answered, quite shyly for me.

'What room are you in?'

'Nile House, room one.'

'Oh wow,' Gemini said. 'We are in the same room, what are the chances?'

A girl with thick glasses sitting across the aisle leant over. 'Statistically speaking, there is a really good chance that someone here will be in your—'

Someone in the back shouted, 'Harmattan!'

There was a sudden cry of 'Harmattan!

Harmattan! Harmattan! Hey hey!'

What was going on? I looked at Lola and Gemini for answers.

'Yeah, that's just Tayo. We shout *harmattan* when someone says something as dry as bonga fish,' Gemini explained. 'You know, dry like the harmattan winds that blow from the Sahara desert!'

Lola burst into her howling laughter. I couldn't help joining in. The way Gemini said 'bonga fish' with an American accent was so funny.

'Technically, bonga fish is not—'

Tayo was interrupted by a loud whistle from outside the coach.

'Matron!' somebody whispered.

I looked out of my window to see a large woman with short grey hair. She had hard, piercing eyes that looked like they had never been affected by a smile. She was dressed smartly in a pale blue uniform with several silver badges attached. She looked very important indeed.

The whistle made all the seniors round up their conversations with the Kingswill boys. As the older girls started coming into the coach, there was a gentle tap at my window. I turned to look, as did all the other girls around me. I nearly died when I saw Owolabi. He was grinning from ear to ear. I wanted to sink into my seat and disappear. Lola jumped up.

'Oooh, it's my cousin, Owolabi!' she yelped, reaching past me to push down the coach window. I sat up more comfortably now that I knew I wasn't the one he wanted to see. Gemini and the other girls started making a huge fuss over him.

'Aw, he's so cute,' Gemini gushed.

'Look at his round cheeks,' another girl said.

They must be barking mad, I thought.

'Jummy!' His voice sounded strangely deeper than usual.

'Yes?' I said, rolling my eyes and hoping he wouldn't say anything annoying.

He handed me a piece of paper through the window, and all the girls whooped as if he had given me gold. I grabbed it from him and went back to sinking into my seat. I was mortified. I opened it to find his address scrawled on the paper.

Kingswill College
Private Mail Box 110
Ogun State, Nigeria

Lola had just snatched the paper off me and was going to mock me some more, I was sure, but Senior Moradeke stood up to do a roll call. Everyone waved frantically at Owolabi as he disappeared back to his coach, and I used the roll call as an excuse to close the window and face forwards. My name was one of the first to be called as I was in Nile House, room one.

'Here!' I shouted clearly.

'Bolaji Oni,' Senior Moradeke called, but nobody responded.

'She hasn't arrived yet. We may have to leave without her,' Mrs Aliu said, shaking her head in disapproval.

But just as the roll call was finished, Tayo cried out, 'Ma, look at those four big cars just coming, there is a girl in orange housewear inside one of them.'

'Ah, that must be Bolaji Oni, the girl who almost didn't make it.'

The four cars parked on my side of the coach. Everyone watched as two large soldiers came out of the last two cars and stood guard. A driver stepped out of the second car and ran round to open the door for a man dressed in an all-white guinea with a brocade agbada flowing to the ground. He wore dark sunglasses and a dark green traditional Yoruba cap with several insignia. He looked like a prince!

'These must be the Oni royal family who own Redbrick Bakery!' Tayo announced.

Several girls from the other side of the coach came squeezing through to our side to get a closer look. The driver went to the third car to open the door. Out stepped a girl in what was supposed to be Nile housewear, only it looked like a party dress. Her white blouse had puffy sleeves and a collar that stood up straight just like its wearer. She was about my size, but she walked as though someone pulled her head from above and her nose was so pointed it looked like it could be used to pierce ears. She ran to the man in the flowing agbada, hugged him and wouldn't let go.

Mrs Aliu sucked her teeth in irritation and

got off the coach.

As she approached the newcomers, so did Matron and a tall, bespectacled senior girl in purple-checked skirt and blouse. I tried to remember what the purple house was. Limpopo, I thought.

While Mrs Aliu and Matron spoke to the prince, the new girl climbed back into the car. The Limpopo senior looked at us with a scowl that made all of us pretend not to be interested.

There seemed to be an endless conversation that we couldn't hear, but you could tell there was a disagreement of some sort. Matron looked very angry with Mrs Aliu.

'We can settle this when we get to the school.' Mrs Aliu's voice was suddenly piercing.

After a few more moments of difficult conversation, the girl finally got out of the car and on to the coach with Mrs Aliu. Her eyes were swollen and red. She looked away and found a seat at the front. Matron was still standing outside talking to the senior girl in purple, her arms folded and looking very displeased indeed.

Lola nudged me and whispered, 'This one is going to have fun at the River School.'

The coach roared to life and started to reverse out of the station. As soon as it was on the move, the girls began to chant and point towards the driver.

Baba Wale, show us your driving power!
God be with us this hour!

There were many other strange songs that the girls sang. I couldn't help feeling lost. When would I know the words and be able to join in? Lola was so full of life and had so many friends. I didn't even know who was in my class.

How was I ever going to manage?

I must have fallen asleep because Lola was nudging me.

'Wake up, Jumoke, we are almost there. The Redbrick Bakery is coming up on the left. Once you see that, you know the River School is only five minutes away.'

'Redbrick Bakery is the largest bakery in Nigeria with several branches across the country.'

I stared politely at Tayo, the dry bonga fish girl, as she rolled off more information.

'They bake over a hundred thousand loaves of bread a day and even the Sultan of Sokoto has been known to order his bread from Redbrick.'

Gemini shouted from the back. 'Jumoke, you better get used to Tayo, she never stops.'

Everyone laughed and I wondered if Tayo would be upset, but when I peeked across at her, she was laughing too and I admired her for being able to laugh at herself.

The massive bakery was a welcome change of scenery from the vast countryside. It was painted a bright scarlet and white with REDBRICK BAKERY in capital letters. As we drove past, the unmistakable smell of freshly baked bread wafted through the air. My tummy growled. It smelt just like Auntie Heather's fresh bread and chinchin.

'Ah, Redbrick Bakery, I have missed you,' a girl cried out.

'Grubido!' someone shouted back.

'Sharap!' she yelled in response.

Everyone hooted again. I laughed too. I had heard Caro say 'shut up' many times like that to ThankGod.

The coach mounted a bridge and the girls went quiet for a full ten seconds. I looked out of the window and saw why. We were driving over the most captivating river you ever saw. It glistened in the sunlight and there were canoes and fishermen casting nets. It was like once we were on that bridge, everything mellowed.

'An angel is passing by,' someone whispered.

'Shine-Shine River?' I whispered to Lola, not wanting to spoil the mood.

She nodded back at me and smiled.

'Leke Leke!' she said, pointing to a flock of white egrets flying low over the river. *Leke Leke* was the Yoruba word.

Many of the girls started chanting softly.

> *Leke Leke bami leke*
> *Eye atata bami leke*
> *Leke Leke, give me white fingernails*
> *Leke Leke, give me white fingernails*

This time, I was able to join in. I remembered long trips to see Grandma and Grandpa in Ekiti. There were so many Leke Leke along the rivers we passed and I believed that if I sang the Leke Leke song to them, I would get white spots on my fingernails. Sometimes I got them, sometimes I didn't, but I always made sure I didn't already have the white spots before I got into the car.

Once we were off the bridge, the girls began to chat again. The coach went down a long, winding road that was surrounded by a thick forest of tall mahogany trees. Finally, we approached the gates to the River School and they swung open before us as if to say 'welcome home'. They were bright green and white with the words 'Welcome to the River School' on a metal sign at the top. As we passed through, a man sitting in a little wooden booth waved us on with his cap. Lola whispered, 'That's Baba Green!' as if it were some state secret. I shrugged and looked back at the man who was now standing outside the booth, his lanky frame not easily disappearing into the distance. The coach continued up another narrow, winding road with thick bushes and more enormous trees on either side. Lola threw herself past me to push the coach window down.

'Smell the air!' she squealed.

I took a deep breath. All around were the aromas of lemon, mango, guava and agbalumo. I squealed in excitement and Lola giggled.

As we came out of the trees, Lola began to point more things out, her voice full of eagerness.

'That way leads to the staff quarters . . . Those are the playing fields where we play football and hockey . . . That is where me and the girls had a picnic last summer, under those big trees. There's a pond there too!'

The coach stopped in front of a large manicured square with massive palm trees surrounding it. Dead centre was the cutest little white cottage with a front garden that was brilliantly lush, with red hibiscus and yellow allamanda flowers surrounding the greenest lawn I'd ever seen. I imagined myself lying on the soft grass and basking in the glorious sunshine, scoffing down ice-cold ginger ale and chinchin . . .

Lola must have seen the longing in my eyes. 'That's Princey's cottage! It's at the centre of the whole school. All roads lead to it!'

A tall and very impressive woman came out of the cottage. She was dressed in a bright yellow kaftan and matching head tie. Everyone started to wave. I wanted to be in her good books right away.

A black-and-white cat appeared by her side. It put its back up protectively and its tail swayed haughtily.

'Our good old principal!' Lola said as the woman waved back.

'And Barky!' Gemini and Tayo said at the same time.

What a strange name for a cat, I thought.

'You'll soon meet Barky, she comes into the dorms and dining hall!' Lola was already getting out of her seat.

'We missed you, Princey!' Gemini was shouting and waving.

Someone was about to raise another song but Mrs Aliu was having none of it. Our coach joined some others in a lay-by just opposite the cottage. They were already empty.

'Quickly girls, it looks like we are the last ones to arrive. Collect all your things and go straight to your dorms. New girls, follow the older girls and you'll be fine!' Mrs Aliu was looking really tired indeed. Her piercing voice had reduced to a squeak.

We all got off the coach and followed the swarm of excited, chattering girls down the road. Before long we passed another cottage similar in style to Princey's, but it was painted the kind of white that your mother wouldn't let you touch after eating oily puffpuff.

'What's this building?' I asked Lola.

'Oh, that's the sickbay. You don't want to go there unless you're really ill. Matron does not like time-wasters.'

I couldn't help noticing the freshness of the air at the River School. The smell of citrus and freshly cut grass hung heavy and there were lots of orange and lemon trees dotted around. The sounds were different too. At home, I could always hear car horns, hawkers or a running tap. I could only hear the crickets at night when the world had gone to sleep, but I could hear them now trying to rival the racket of the girls.

I also couldn't wait to see the dorms but my bags were heavy and I kept having to stop to re-adjust my load. I had to wheel my suitcase, carry my travel bag on my shoulder and use my other hand to carry my bucket, which kept toppling over from the weight of my broom, cutlass and hoe. Lola, on the other hand, was carrying her things with great ease. There were girls going by with nothing but their travel bags on their shoulders.

'Those are senior girls and they will turn you into their maids if you let them. We are going to have to make ourselves scarce.' Lola stepped up her speed.

'I can't wait to be a senior just for that!'

Lola shook her head disapprovingly.

We turned left and continued for quite a while down a long concrete walkway. There was only just enough path to lead you where you were going. The rest of the grounds were either manicured grass, wild bush or sandy rock. Lizards of various colours leapt up and down the pathways undisturbed by us all.

At last Lola stopped in front of two rows of different-coloured cottages. There were six in total. Each one was painted in a different colour with the name of each house painted neatly in big black letters so you could see from afar which house was which. They looked like those colourful peppermints that were given out at parties.

'Nile is first of course, because it is the best house ever! Look how unique our orange is, just like agbalumo.' Lola was beaming with pride.

Niger was next door to Nile and painted a pale

green, then Senegal, which was sky blue. On the opposite side, across the grass, were Congo which was yellow, then Zambezi which was red and lastly, Limpopo which was purple and stood directly opposite Nile House as if it were challenging it to a duel.

'Just look at how overgrown the quadrangle is!' Lola spread her arms out in front of her for dramatic effect. She was talking about the large squares of bush that divided the houses. It was very unlike Princey's courtyard and full of weeds, and I did not imagine myself lying down in that.

'When are they going to tidy it up?' I asked.

Lola let out her shriek of a laugh and patted my head as she led me inside Nile House.

'I suppose you think you are carrying a hoe and cutlass for a fashion parade?'

I looked at her incredulously. Would I really be expected to do manual labour?

'Let's get inside so we can unpack and choose the best beds.'

CHAPTER EIGHT
NILE HOUSE, ROOM ONE

We climbed the steps that led into Nile House. I dragged my things up in three trips. We were now standing on a large square porch with two white doors on either side. I could see through the deep-orange perforated brick holes in the middle.

The doors opened on to corridors on both sides which surrounded a lawn. There was a flower bed at each end and everything was overgrown like the quadrangle outside. The lawn had drain gutters surrounding it. I walked over and peered into one and saw it was green with algae. I wrinkled my nose. It smelt bad.

Room one was the first of eight doors along one of the long corridors. I walked all the way along to the end. The last door was labelled 'box room'. The corridor on the other side was identical except the last room was labelled 'house captain'.

One of the doors opened and Lola pulled me back towards my room.

'Honestly, Jumoke, we are going to get rotten beds!'

There was a list on my room door.

Nile House, Room One
Funmi Bankole – Form 5 (Deputy house captain)
Ngozi Nwobi – Form 4
Tope Lawanson – Form 3
Gemini Miller – Form 2
Bolaji Oni – Form 1
Jumoke Afolabi – Form 1

'Oh, Her Majesty too!' Lola pointed to Bolaji's name. 'You are so lucky you are in a prefect's room with only six girls. There are ten of us in my room. Four more people to annoy me.' She knocked on the door.

'Come in,' sang a voice from inside.

'Good afternoon, Senior Funmi. This is my family friend, Jumoke Afolabi, she is in your room.'

'Hello, fine girl. Eiya! See how small you are. Come and meet the rest of your room-mates.'

I had hoped my size would not be noticed here, but there was a sing-song quality to Senior Funmi's voice which matched her soft, bright face and I couldn't help liking her immediately.

She jumped down from her top bunk. She was petite and her face was pixie-like. She had beautiful skin that glowed and her cornrows were finely woven in shuku style, all pointing to the top. In her smart orange-checked skirt and blouse, she looked every bit the part of deputy house captain as the badge on her chest declared.

There were two other bunk beds and a girl on almost every bed.

'Everyone, say hello to Jumoke Afolabi.'

Gemini jumped off her top bunk to shake hands with me.

'I'm Gemini but hey, you already knew that.'

I grinned at her. 'Great to meet you too, Gemini.'

Lola kissed her teeth deeply. 'Mschew! Don't let Gemini get you into trouble o, Jumoke.'

'I'm sure if I offer you jollof rice now you will change your tune.' Gemini was tapping the locker beside her. Her huge suitcase lay open before us.

'Ehn, do you have J-rice?' Lola's eyes were now sparkling with interest.

'Cooked food is not allowed in the dorm.' Senior Funmi was looking sternly at Lola.

'Erm, but it was Gemini that mentioned jollof rice. I . . . err, I . . .'

Everyone started laughing. I wasn't sure I could join in yet.

'Hmph!' Someone sighed loudly from the bottom bunk beside Senior Funmi's. It was covered with a large tie-dye cloth at the corners so that it looked like a tent. I noticed feet wearing white plimsolls sticking out at the end of the bed and thought she must be very tall. It shocked me that she was wearing shoes in bed but they looked so clean I didn't judge her.

'Somewhere behind that is Ngozi.'

Gemini was mouthing some words to me but I couldn't make out what she was saying.

'And that's Tope who is my bunkmate.'

The last girl rolled her eyes and took her gaze off the novel she was reading for a few seconds. 'Hello, sorry I can't get up – I get sick when I travel long distances.' She put the book down and clutched her tummy. Her dark brown face and big brown eyes reminded me of Caro and I smiled warmly.

'Imaginary sickness!' Ngozi said, emerging from the tent finally. She was immaculate in a pair of white shorts, an orange Nile House sports T-shirt and the white plimsolls. She had also rolled up the sleeves of her T-shirt so that it looked sleeveless. Her arms had muscles and her stomach was as flat as a pancake. Her skin was shiny black and her afro stood so tall that I couldn't take my eyes off her.

'OK, choose a bed,' Ngozi ordered, pointing to the only two that were empty. One above hers and one under Gemini's.

Gemini and Lola pushed me simultaneously towards Gemini's bunk.

'She chooses this one.' Gemini was smiling as she put her arm around me. 'I think you'll find me to be perfectly awesome, even if I say so myself.'

I was so chuffed to be sharing a bunk with her.

'Suit yourself,' Ngozi said and went straight back behind her tent.

I was worried I might have offended her, but I soon forgot as Lola helped me open my suitcase. She laid my bed with white sheets and pillow-cases, and the orange-checked bedspread that Senior Moradeke had given me earlier. It was part of the rules. No coloured sheets, only white and house-checked bedspreads. But I was the only one in my room with the correct sheets.

When Lola left, I sat on my bed and tried to fit all my things into the small wooden locker assigned to me. I looked at Gemini's locker beside mine. It was wide open and full to the brim with all sorts of soaps and creams that were packaged differently to Nigerian things. She also had lots of cookies and sticky-looking snacks which were definitely not allowed at the River School. I wondered how she could be so brazen with a prefect in our room.

There were several girls coming in and out, mostly to see Senior Funmi, whose bunk was directly opposite mine. Everyone kept asking where the other Form One girl was.

'Ah, I don't know o!' Senior Funmi would reply in a straightforward manner.

'She is inside my nose!' Ngozi would flick one nostril up in response if anyone dared to ask her.

Senior Funmi's friends all talked really loudly and were full of exciting stories.

'Funmi! You goat, you didn't come for my birthday party during long hols. You missed big time!'

'We travelled to Abeokuta o. We only got back last week.'

'Ah, Abeokuta! That sounds like a really dry village trip.'

'You know I have lots of cousins there. And besides, Abeokuta is a city, Folashade, not a village!' Senior Funmi still sounded like she was singing even when she was making a point.

I wondered how she was going to loosen her very tiny cornrows and what would happen if Ngozi didn't plait hers. Everyone who wore their hair long had to have it in at least two plaits for classes.

Senior Funmi brought out an album from her locker and showed her friends pictures. They giggled together. It reminded me of Owolabi and his huge album of photos that he had taken with his Polaroid. Sometimes Caro, Owolabi, ThankGod and I would gather under the fruit tree to look at pictures. I suddenly felt a wave of emotion and wanted to be back at home.

Most of the girls had left the room now. The noise out in the corridors was fierce. I wished I could join in. I opened my travelling bag slowly, looking around to see if anyone was looking my way. There was something wrapped in foil. I hoped with all my heart that it was Mummy's fried chicken. She dipped it in milk and bread-crumbs before frying it and it was so delicious.

No sooner had the foil squeaked than Gemini was jumping down from the top bunk above me, her strong legs bashing my head as she did so.

'What have you got there?' She stood in front of me, one hand on her hip and the other jingling her keys. Her unruly curls had now totally un-ravelled from her cornrows and were hanging for dear life in a fat orange hair band. Her face was very mischievous with large, daring eyes.

'I haven't looked inside yet.'

'Go on then.'

I opened it. It was Mummy's fried chicken.

Gemini gasped. 'Oh wow, it's like my mother's chicken. Where are you from?'

'Lagos.'

'Well, my mom's from Illinois but from the looks of your mom's cooking, we are going to have a great time together, you and me. I bet we have loads in common.' She looked around and whispered, 'Don't eat it yet. A few of us have plans for tonight.'

I pinched a piece from a chicken wing and wrapped the rest up. I didn't want to miss out on anything!

CHAPTER NINE

FIRST NIGHT

We spent the rest of the evening chatting and reliving summer stories. My summer had not been the same without Caro, I thought. By the time the bell rang for lights out, I was already nodding off.

I must have been asleep for some time when I heard Gemini whispering my name and shining a torch in my eye.

'Jumoke, wake up, follow me and bring your delicious chicken.'

I was trying to make sense of what she was saying when I saw she had a large food flask and a school bag in her hands. I grabbed my foil from my bag and followed her.

She walked all the way to the end of the corridor and into the large box room where I had carried my suitcase after unpacking.

There were about seven other girls in their nightshirts sitting on suitcases with a woolly blanket on the floor, which was covered with different kinds of food.

Several candles were lit and stuck with wax on upside-down metal buckets. There were torches on the blanket and I could see jollof rice and lots of my favourite snacks.

Lola must have been right behind us because she pushed us into the room.

'What did you bring, Gemini?' She was trying to pull the food flask from Gemini's hands.

'I've got more jollof rice and Oreo cookies.' She raised the flask and bag up in the air dramatically.

There was a loud hum of approval as Gemini tipped over the bag on to the blanket to reveal packets of Oreo cookies, sticky sweets and other sweet-looking things I had never seen before. She opened up the flask and threw several plastic forks on to the blanket. A few girls started to tuck into the rice.

'What did JJC bring? Statistics show that JJCs generally don't know what to bring,' Tayo declared, her thick glasses clinging desperately to the tip of her nose.

Before I could ask what JJC meant, Lola grabbed my foil. 'This JJC knows exactly what to bring! Gosh! I hope it's your mummy's fantastic fried chicken.'

Gemini leant in as if she had read my mind. 'JJC stands for Johnny Just Come.'

'Who's Johnny?' I asked naively.

Everyone nearly choked with laughter. I joined them knowing it would take me a while to understand their slang.

'It is your mum's delicious chicken!' Lola cried out with so much enthusiasm that one of the girls had to cover her mouth with her palm.

'Lola Fernando, shut up! You want to get us into trouble with Senior Moradeke?'

Several of the girls started giggling.

I sat down on a plastic bucket that Tayo had turned over for me. I tried to make out the girls' faces. It was difficult because all the torches and candles were aimed at shining light on the food. I must say the spread looked really good. There was puffpuff, chinchin, plantain chips and meat pies. My stomach growled and everyone heard it and laughed again.

A white girl wearing glasses just like Tayo's turned to me and said, 'So do you like the River School so far? How different is it to where you live? Where *do* you live?' Her accent sounded French.

I didn't know which question to answer first.

'I'm Michelle,' the girl went on, without waiting for my reply. 'My mother is Madame Celestine who teaches us French. Me and Tayo, we are twins as you can see, no?'

'Only, one asks too many questions and the other answers questions nobody asked her!' Gemini butted in.

There was a roar of giggles!

Apart from the fact that both girls wore the exact same rectangular glasses, they could not have been more different. Tayo was round and short with cheeks that looked as if they had been stuffed with puffpuff, and Michelle was tall and thin. Tayo had tightly braided plaits that she parted into two ponytails with a small fringe of plaits, and Michelle also had her long black hair plaited into two with a small fringe. Twins indeed.

Michelle repeated all her questions. So I tried to answer them.

'I live in Lagos and—'

'So you must love it here! No noise!' she interrupted. 'My family live just outside the school but I prefer to be in the dorms with everyone.'

Tayo jumped up. 'Of course you prefer to live with us. A recent poll says the River School is the best school in Southern Nigeria, you know? It showed that we have had the highest West Africa Examination results for the last seven years!' Some of the other girls groaned.

'What about Kingswill College next door?' I blurted out. I don't know why I said that and I wanted to take the words back straight away, but it was too late. Everyone, apart from a tiny little girl sitting on a metal bucket with a pillow on it, attacked me.

'Oooooh!' they all shrieked in unison.

'You are in the hot stew now!' Michelle said in between munches of chinchin.

Tayo laughed. 'It's hot soup, Michelle, not "the hot stew"!'

Gemini was wagging her finger at me and shaking her head like an agama lizard.

Lola came to my rescue. 'Girls, keep your voices down. Baba Green may be on the prowl.'

'Better than Matron!' Michelle said.

'Yes! Baba Green does not know our names, Matron knows everybody,' Tayo added.

'But Baba Green can turn you into a crocodile!' Gemini insisted. This caused everyone to erupt with laughter.

'Is that the gate man we saw earlier?' I asked.

Tayo shuffled up beside me. 'He is the gate man, the gardener and the shuttle bus driver.'

'Also, he helped me break open my padlock when I lost my key,' Michelle declared.

'Although, Baba Green at night is not the same as Baba Green in the daytime!' Gemini jumped up to make her point. 'He once rode a crocodile like a canoe along the river and all the girls saw him the next day wearing crocodile boots. Nobody has actually seen his face at night! Except in your nightmares where he returns with red eyes and a green kaftan, chasing you!'

'Gemini! Stop scaring the poor JJCs with rumours! Why don't you get to know the Form One girl in my room?' Lola nudged me towards the only other tiny girl in the room.

I thought she may even be smaller than I was. I sat on the metal portmanteau beside her. My mum had almost bought one for me but Lola's mum had insisted it would be the most common box in the school. There were several of the same mounted on each other.

'I'm Bukky.' She held out her hand towards me. 'I'm in Form One O and I'm in Lola's room.' She smiled to reveal large white teeth that seemed bigger than normal. Several of them were jumbled up and even growing through her gums.

'I'm in Form One O as well.' I liked her already. She was small like me and seemed friendly.

I grabbed some chinchin and tossed them into my mouth. I was expecting a little crunch, then a soft middle, but it was all crunch and my teeth hurt. I nearly spat it out. Lola let out a shriek of merriment that got everyone going.

'Sssssh!' someone whispered loudly.

A dark shadow flitted across the window. Then the sound of footsteps and a light tapping.

'Baba Green!' a few girls said in unison.

The whole room went eerily quiet. Torches were quenched and candles snuffed out. You could smell the wax as it wafted through the room and a shadow-like figure passed by the second window. I was so scared, I thought I'd wet myself. I could not see anyone's face but I could hear the toads and crickets making a racket outside.

Gemini started singing softly, 'Baba Green can make you crawl crawl like crocodile.'

The other girls whispered in response:

Crawl crawl like crocodile
Crawl crawl like crocodile!

Gemini was about to continue but I heard a little thud and then she let out a cry. There were muffled giggles as Lola went to peek through the window.

'He's gone. Let's go to bed o.'

The girls started to clear up. Everyone grabbed

some food to take away.

When we got back to our room, everyone was fast asleep but the bed above Ngozi's was still empty. I wondered where Bolaji was. As I crept into my bed, I kicked a metal bucket. The pain in my little toe was excruciating and I leapt in wincing from the pain.

'Who is that?' Senior Funmi whispered.

'It's me,' Gemini said quickly. 'I went to the toilet.'

'OK, go back to bed.'

Gemini whispered something to me but I couldn't make out what it was. I was still nursing my toe. When the pain subsided I lay awake for a while wondering what Baba and Mummy would be doing now. It was just after midnight and I bet Baba would say that he hadn't fallen asleep watching TV when Mummy woke him up. He would go right back to sleep clutching the remote control, his head bobbing up and down with all the channels closed and only showing the multi-coloured stripes.

An owl was making soft noises outside my window. I thought of Caro and her noisy cockerel and wondered how she was. Was she back from visiting Big Auntie? Would she reply to my letters? Would she remember me when she looked up into the night sky?

CHAPTER TEN
FIRST MORNING

I woke to the sound of someone dragging her metal bucket.

'Stop making noise, Tope!'

'Sorry, Senior Funmi, I just wanted to get a private shower cubicle before the bell goes.'

'You must have turned into a senior girl overnight.'

Gemini giggled under her covers.

'No, Senior Funmi, I'm on my period and . . .'

'Just go and have your shower.'

The wake-up bell went at exactly 6.30 a.m. I was slowly sitting up when a loud cry went out. 'All Forms One to Four girls on to the lawn now!'

Before I could say anything, Gemini and Tope jumped out of their beds and ran out of the room. I followed them down the corridor towards the lawn.

It was quite dark outside and you could hear several crickets chirping as if to encourage us to wake up. I could just make out faces from the lights streaming on to the grass from the bedrooms. Many had tied their wrappers around their waists or over their shoulders. I hadn't done that. I just followed my room-mates and made sure I stuck close to them. The morning air was chilly.

Unlike the rest of us, Senior Moradeke, our Nile House captain, was already washed and dressed in her crisp khaki-green skirt and starched white shirt. She peered down at us with her small dark eyes. They were the only things small about her. She had heavily set cheekbones and a strong jawline that made you know she meant business. She'd be the person I'd want in my corner if I ever got into trouble.

'This is a new term,' Senior Moradeke declared. 'Nile House will change from being an average house to the best house. Do you understand?'

'Yes!' we all cried with surprising enthusiasm, given the time of day.

'Morning duties will be assigned later today after the prefects are officially announced at assembly. For this morning, all Form One girls will sweep and tidy their rooms. Form Two and Three girls will be in charge of gutters and toilets.'

There was a loud groan and Senior Moradeke shouted, 'All Form Two and Three girls, on your knees!'

I saw Lola and Gemini drop down obediently.

'Please, Senior Moradeke, I can't kneel down,' said Tope, who was wearing only a towel. 'I have MP.'

Everyone started laughing. I knew that stood for menstrual pain.

'Tope Lawanson! Save that for your drama club. Something is always wrong with you. I don't have time for you this morning.'

'As I was saying, Form Two and Three girls are in charge of gutters and toilets. You are even lucky there is running water or it would have been straight to the borehole for all of you.' There was silence, as no one wanted to join the girls on their knees.

'Form Four girls will be supervising the work but also in charge of bathrooms.'

'Please make sure you lay your beds with the correct bedspreads. You are dismissed!'

There was a loud shuffling of feet as we all left to do our work and get ready for the day. Gemini was off like a flash.

'What's the hurry?' I said as I tried to catch up with her.

'We have to be quick to get a space around the lawn to wash.'

'The lawn?'

'Yes, the lawn. There are only twelve bathrooms and usually they're for Form Four and Five girls. We have to bathe on the concrete path around the lawn.'

I did not really understand how we would do this but I got on with cleaning our bedroom.

Senior Funmi began to chuckle. 'Do you sweep at home?'

'Yes, but I normally use a long brush, not this

kind of broom made from palm fronds.'

'Ah, ajebutter girl. You have to bend down low to get all the dirt.' She held out her hand to show me. I nodded my head in agreement. I had seen Joy sweep enough times. I didn't want anyone to start calling me a spoilt girl who couldn't sweep floors.

I bent down well and swept with all my might, but when everyone left the room to have their baths, I got tired. I wished there was someone to help me. I looked to see if anyone was coming and then swept all the dust under my locker. That was when Gemini put her head around the door.

I stood up very straight holding the broom behind me.

'What are you up to?' She looked at me suspiciously.

'Nothing! Have you done your morning duty?' I asked, trying to change the topic.

'Yup! Let's go and bath.' Gemini shrugged.

I brought my bucket from underneath my bed and grabbed my green towel which hung from the top bunk railing. I followed Gemini out of the room and into the corridor.

'I knew it! We should have come earlier. There's no space.' Gemini crashed her really large bucket of water down wildly, letting it spill. If Caro was here, she would have said, *My friend, stop wasting water!*

There were about eight girls by the lawn with buckets of water in front of them. They were washing themselves right there in the open space! There were also about ten of us waiting to take their places once they finished.

'Here, take some of my water. There is no use going to fetch water at that dirty sink area.' She began to empty about a quarter of her bucket into mine.

'I hope you know how to manage water, Jummy.'

'I certainly do!' I said.

The girls already on the lawn tied their towels like head ties on their heads because there was nowhere else to put them. Most had small buckets like mine with their names boldly printed in markers on them. They were different colours, mostly plastic but some were metal. Mummy said a metal bucket was too heavy and harsh to carry so I got plastic, and orange too.

The girls bathing were very careful with the water, not pouring it over themselves with large bowls like I did at home. Only when they had soaped themselves completely, did they use the water to rinse.

One of the girls started to wash her face and so had her eyes shut. Gemini nudged me. She drew my attention to the other girls by raising her eyebrows. They started to quietly take bowls of water out of the bucket belonging to the girl who had her eyes shut. I looked on horrified. I couldn't imagine what she would do. She was covered in soap from head to toe. Did she even have any water left to rinse herself? The clanging sound made by her bowl as it hit the bottom of her metal bucket answered my question.

She shrieked. 'Oh come on, guys! What is this?'

Gemini's laugh filled the air. She looked at me and her American accent was at its peak when she whispered, 'Rookie mistake made by an oldie!'

We moved into the spaces that had become available and Gemini called over to the girl covered in soap.

'Hey, Pat! I'll give you two bowls of water for your afternoon snack tomorrow.'

'It's not funny, Gemini. Help me out.'

'Two bowls, one afternoon snack.' Gemini was beaming at me.

'OK, three bowls.' Pat held out her empty bowl.

'Deal!'

I don't know how Gemini managed the little water she now had but when it came to washing my face, I kept my eyes wide open.

Though it was Monday, I dressed in my Sunday white dress because new girls were to go to their classes and receive their books and uniforms from their class teachers. I watched the other girls dress smartly in their khaki-green dresses and white collars and belts. I couldn't wait to get mine. The Form Four and Five girls were even smarter in their white cotton shirts tucked into green skirts.

We were just leaving for breakfast when Ngozi emerged from her self-made tent, still in her undergarments but her hair now beautifully twisted.

'Someone better bring my food out of the dining room,' she shouted after us, 'and drop it in my class before assembly, or else!'

We didn't say a word.

'Ngozi! Nobody here is your maid o!' Senior Funmi said, shaking her head.

'Maybe by the end of today, you won't be the only prefect in this room!' Ngozi snapped.

I wasn't sure who I feared more, Baba Green or Ngozi.

The dining hall was made of burnt-orange brick and its roof hung over it like a rice picker's hat. Nothing prepared me for the vastness inside. There seemed to be endless rows of wooden tables with long benches on either side.

The noise was on another level. Everyone was moving up and down the aisles carrying crockery and chatting with friends who they hadn't seen since last term.

Gemini was walking briskly ahead of me. I followed her towards the Nile House tables – a large orange beam marked the area. A mixture of body heat and fresh air from the several doorless entrances hit me from different directions. I could detect the faint aroma of fresh bread trying to triumph over the different smells.

Gemini yelled above the noise as we sat down. 'You will soon see how awesome it is to be at the front of the room, Jum-Jum. You can get your tea first and leave straight away. Even when there is extra food, you get it first.'

I smiled at her. I loved how she was constantly giving me new names. Gemini had not stopped talking since we left our dorm.

Senior Moradeke came to the front of the dining hall. She held her hands behind her back and said nothing. It was like a magic spell had been cast on us all. She was so formidable and precise, nobody dared utter a sound. I could hear birds chirping outside.

'All stand,' she bellowed.

We all got to our feet.

'For the food we are about to receive, we thank thee, o Lord.'

'Amen,' we said in unison.

Gemini stood up to serve the food on our table. Tope distributed the plates to no one in particular and started to open the loaves of sliced bread. They had the words REDBRICK BAKERY stamped all over the wrapping.

Senior Funmi and Ngozi joined us at the table, laughing like best mates.

Gemini opened the pot and used the large stainless steel serving spoon to evenly distribute fish stew. It was red with chunks of fish, and looked nice but a bit watery. In any case, it didn't matter – I was starving.

Tope put five slices of bread on each plate.

'E wa jeun!' She made an exaggerated curtsey, inviting us to tuck in!

I waited to see what others would do. Senior Funmi came to my rescue.

'Jumoke, just take the plate in front of you.'

'Looks like you are lucky today, Gemini – or perhaps someone served you a big portion on purpose,' Ngozi said.

'I served everyone the same.' Gemini scowled.

'You don't say,' Ngozi drawled.

Tope laughed. 'You should join our drama club, Ngozi, your American accent is good o!'

From the Limpopo end of the hall, I could see a

host of girls coming towards us. I recognized Bolaji and the Limpopo senior who seemed to be the leader of the pack. She looked even more immaculate than Senior Moradeke. She wore a bright green cardigan over her uniform and short brown boots instead of sandals, which made her look different from everyone. Her walk was dripping with confidence and it must have rubbed off on Bolaji, who looked very impressive in her white dress. It was satin and it shimmered in the dining-hall light. She seemed so different from the girl with red eyes on the coach yesterday. I didn't imagine I would be friends with her. She seemed so extra.

Ngozi and Senior Funmi looked up as the group approached.

'Hello, Alero,' Senior Funmi said mildly.

'What's with the entourage?' Ngozi added.

The six girls that had accompanied them looked down at their school shoes. Bolaji kept her head up.

'I came to collect my cousin's food!' said Alero, the Limpopo senior. 'This is Bolaji, she is in your room apparently but there's been a mistake. She is supposed to be in Limpopo. In a matter of days, Matron will send her purple housewear.'

Ngozi attempted to stand but Senior Funmi stopped her.

'Listen, Alero!' she said firmly. 'Bolaji will eat here until that mistake is cleared up. In fact, she must report to her room in Nile House by the end of classes today. I am deputy house captain and I insist on it!'

Bolaji's mouth dropped.

'Don't worry, Bolaji,' Alero said. 'Matron will soon sort this nonsense out and in any case, I'm sure you can stay with her any time you get tired of this dirty Nile!'

This time Ngozi stood up. She towered over the entourage and Alero. The tension between the two senior girls was intense.

'I'll leave you for now but I'll be back for Bolaji!' Alero snapped her fingers, the entourage giggled briefly and then they were gone, leaving Bolaji on her own to face us.

She lifted her chin, took her food and sat down beside Tope.

Gemini and I tried to keep ourselves from

bursting out in giggles.

'My family owns Redbrick Bakery, you know,' she said. 'At home, we eat our bread straight from chef's oven, fresh and hot, not like this.' Bolaji picked up two slices of bread and dropped them again. She looked around the table.

Nobody said anything so she just stared down at her plate defiantly, eating nothing.

I tore my first slice and dipped a bit into the stew, and then I looked at everyone else.

'Jumoke, just put all the stew on one slice and make a giant sandwich, like this,' Gemini whispered to me while eating her own enormous one.

'Won't it make the bread soggy?'

'Try it,' Senior Funmi said.

I tried it. It was delicious. The other four slices made it just perfect.

I was almost finished when Senior Moradeke shouted out again. 'For the food we have just received, we thank thee, o Lord.'

'Amen!' we all shouted back but this time everyone raced out of the hall. Gemini pulled me up.

'Quick, Jum-Jum – no one's been assigned duties yet, so last ones out clear the plates!'

I grabbed my school bag and what was left of my sandwich and we ran to meet Lola!

CHAPTER TWELVE

FIRST ASSEMBLY

The sun had now risen boldly into the sky but the grass was still moist from the night's dew. I dug my brown leather shoes into it, not minding my white socks.

'Do you know what class you are in?' Lola asked as she finished her stew sandwich.

'One O. It says on the letter,' I replied while swallowing the last of mine.

'There are five classes to each year: N, O, P, Q, R, S.' Lola scrunched the Redbrick bread paper into her uniform pocket.

'Random, right?' Gemini laughed.

'Yeah, very random,' I agreed.

Lola continued, 'Mrs Folawiyo, the music teacher, was our class teacher when I was in One O so if you get her, you'll be so lucky. She is so clever and nice. She is Ghanaian and married to Reverend Folawiyo.'

'Well, Reverend is nice too but so, so boring . . .' Gemini yawned exaggeratedly and threw her arms in the air.

I really wished I was in Gemini's class.

'Yup, Rev. Folawiyo can send anyone to sleep,' Lola added.

We were quiet for a while, following the long trail of trees all the way round until we got to a wide-open concrete space with cars parked around the edges. There were already several girls forming lines facing the large building in front of it. It was a grey two-storey building with a dark blue roof that spread across the assembly ground. It had a grand stairway in the front surrounded by lemon, mango and palm trees. Teachers had started to gather on the top of the stairway.

'Look, there's Mrs Folawiyo,' said Gemini. 'Let's find out if she is O's teacher.'

Mrs Folawiyo was so beautiful. Her black skin shone and her hair was set in loose curls falling down her shoulders. She wore a long ankara skirt and a crisp white blouse with frilly sleeves. There was already a large number of girls, both big and small, vying for her attention.

Next to her was a sign that said 'Form One O'. 'Mrs Folawiyo, are you the class teacher for Form One O?' Gemini was practically shrieking, her American accent at full blast.

'No, Gemini, I just feel like standing in front of this sign right here,' she said, smiling.

There was a roar of laughs.

'Oops, I didn't see that! Sorry, Ma.'

'I was trying to tell you that.' I smiled, happy to know something before these Form Two girls for a change.

Mrs Folawiyo smiled at me. 'What is your name?'

'My name is Jumoke Afolabi, Ma.'

'Ah! You are number seven on my list. You will collect your uniform and books from me later this morning and let me know if it is the right size. Some of you are so tiny. OK, find your height and stand in line.'

There were only two girls who were shorter than me and I took my spot behind them.

'See you later,' Lola said as she and Gemini ran to their own line.

A few girls came just before the bell rang. One was almost as tall as Mrs Folawiyo. I heard her say her name was Francesca Davies. She was white and wore her very black hair in a short bob. She went straight to the back of the line.

Bukky arrived and pushed herself in front of me. She flashed her scattered teeth and I smiled back. I was so happy to know someone in my class and to be fourth in line. For a change, I wasn't the smallest.

The bell rang and some teachers came out on to a flight of stairs that spread out from the building in front of the assembly ground.

Princey came to the microphone at the top of the stairs. She towered over all the other teachers and looked really grand in her Yoruba attire of brown-and-white adire. Her red-and-gold head tie was as magnificent as the newscasters' on the seven o'clock news.

'I'm so excited!' Bukky clapped her hands together.

'Ssh!' Mrs Folawiyo gave her a warning look.

'Good morning, girls.' Princey's calm but bold voice boomed from the microphone.

'Good morning, Mrs Ayodele,' everyone chimed. Ah yes, that was the name at the bottom of my admission letter, I recalled.

'It is so good to have you back. Welcome to what I hope will be your best year yet at the River School. We have so much planned for you this term but first let me welcome the Form One girls. Well done for succeeding at your entry exams. We are so excited to have such a talented bunch of girls this year. You are surrounded by beautiful grounds and people that may look and sound very different from home. The question we are asking by providing such an environment is this: what would it look like if all of us came together to help you succeed? This is what it would look like.'

You could hear a pin drop. Princey held out her hands and smiled into the silence. Immediately, the whole school erupted into roaring applause. Everyone began to chant.

Together, we truly shine
For victory is yours and mine
Shine River School, River School shine!

A lump formed in my throat as I realized the applause was for us. They were cheering for the Form One girls. I wanted to impress this lady and show her she had made the right choice accepting me into the River School.

Mrs Ayodele continued to speak. 'Apart from your academic work, we have two major events as part of our half-term activities. One is the annual performance by our Drama and Dance Society and the other is the Harmattan Games, our annual inter-house sports tournament which will take place on the last Saturday of term when your parents are able to visit. Here at the River School we like to say . . .' As she said this, she paused dramatically, smiled and raised her arms towards us. The whole school bellowed in response.

'If you can win in harmattan, you can win in all seasons!'

This time, I joined in the cheering. I was so happy to be part of this school.

Mrs Ayodele continued and silence was restored immediately.

'We are working hard to make sure that all the facilities in our new stadium are ready for the games. There will be an opportunity to try out for the games, so make sure you sign up. With that in mind, I would like to announce this year's prefects and, in particular, the sports captain for each house.'

All the girls cheered as each house's sports captain was announced and I joined in too. I loved watching athletics on TV and sometimes imagined I was Mary Onyali winning gold at the Olympics – my afro blowing in the wind as the crowd screamed my name. But we had never had a proper track at our primary school or the chance to train.

'Limpopo sports captain – Alero Oni.' Another loud applause erupted as Bolaji's cousin walked triumphantly up the stairs to receive her badge. She didn't look so impressive without her bevy of girls behind her.

'Nile House sports captain – Ngozi Nwobi.' This time, there was a louder cheer that seemed to go on for ever. I was surprised. She didn't have many friends from what I had seen. She seemed so contrary.

Ngozi walked up to join the other captains. She was a head taller than all of them and her body, though leaner than the others, looked stronger like a true athlete. A student shouted, 'N-Squared for the River School.' And there was a loud roar.

Mrs Ayodele smiled. 'Yes, Ngozi Nwobi has done our school proud. Last year she won us the gold in cross-country, high jump and long jump in the Southern Nigeria championships. So perhaps this will be the year Nile House wins the Harmattan Games for the first time—'

'That can never happen!' Alero dared to interrupt.

Roars broke out across the assembly ground. Some in agreement, some in protest.

Princey smiled. 'We shall just have to wait and see.'

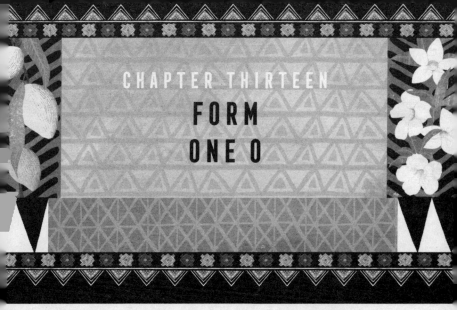

CHAPTER THIRTEEN

FORM ONE O

Nobody seemed to be interested in talking about anything else but Ngozi as we followed Mrs Folawiyo to our classroom. Her name was on everyone's lips.

'She is the fastest thing on two legs,' one girl said.

'She can jump so high, she's like a gazelle!' another replied.

It went on and on.

'Looks like you have a superstar in your room,' Bukky said to me.

'Yeah, looks like it. It makes sense. I think she even arrived in her sports gear.'

'No, I heard she and a few others arrived a week earlier to train with the sports coaches.'

We passed a building called the Great Hall. It was built like a dome but that wasn't the only thing that distinguished it from all the cottage-like buildings at the River School. From the section I could see, it was painted in panels of orange, purple and blue, so I was sure the other end would be green, red and yellow.

'Hey, Pawpaw! Wait for me!' I heard someone say from behind.

We turned round. It was Francesca Davies, the tall girl from the back of our line.

She appeared even taller when she was beside us.

'Hello!' Bukky's face lit up. 'This is Francesca, we went to primary school together in Ibadan. Also, her dad is principal at Kingswill's.'

'You don't have to tell everyone that!' Francesca protested.

'Hello. I'm Jumoke. I saw you when you signed in with the class teacher.' I lifted my arms in the air to show it was her height I had noticed.

'Yup, that's me, Flanky.'

'That's what they called her when she arrived from England because she's so tall and lanky,' Bukky explained, poking Flanky fondly in the tummy. 'And I was Pawpaw! For obvious reasons.'

I looked at her fair complexion and grinned.

'You know we're lucky to be in Nile House?' Flanky said as we made our way to the hall. 'It will be the best house for sports because of Ngozi.'

Bukky quickly butted in. 'Let me just tell you, nothing has changed, Flanky, I still hate sports. I'll make it my life's work to avoid it.' She was suddenly animated. It was a joy to watch, her beaming smile showing her jumbled-up teeth.

Flanky threw her head back and laughed. 'I know you are an efiko in schoolwork but you could be an efiko in sports too, you know?'

'That's where you are wrong. You can't be an expert at both. You can be average, good even, but never an expert.'

I bit my lip as I listened to their banter. Nobody had ever accused me of being an efiko at anything. I wished Caro were here. She was an efiko with numbers and very good at dancing too! What was I good at? I wished I was an efiko at something!

Flanky stopped and ran towards the nearest tree, her short black hair bouncing with her every move. She touched it with her forefinger and ran back to us. She must have seen the amusement in my eyes.

'I'm touching wood. You know, for good luck. I'm going to be chosen to run for Nile House!' she declared.

'Wow, does it work?' I asked, looking at the tree.

Flanky shrugged. 'I'll let you know when luck strikes today!'

Finally, we got to our block of classrooms, which was just like the other blocks we had passed on the way. A set of five cream-colored brick buildings. Ours was marked 'Form One O', the second in line. Mrs Folawiyo was standing outside talking to Mrs Aliu. She looked different today in her long, flowing bubu but I recognized her shrill voice.

Inside the classroom, there were rows of desks and chairs. Thirty of us would be here for the rest of the year. I looked around. All the back desks were taken as well as the window seats. The class had frosted-glass louvre windows all along both sides. Some were open, letting the fresh air through, while some were left shut, keeping the sun out. Bukky dashed towards the front to claim the desk right in front of the blackboard. Flanky went for the one directly behind her. And I sat beside Flanky. We made a kind of triangle with Bukky at the top.

There was a lot of noise from girls dragging their desks or chairs this way and that, trying to get their things in place. Mrs Folawiyo came in and began to speak. The buzz died down immediately.

'Welcome to Form One O. I am Mrs Folawiyo, your class mistress. I teach music, English and home economics. Mrs Aliu is outside waiting to take you in maths. Inside your lockers, you will find all your exercise books, uniforms and time-tables, thanks to the Form Two girls. They have also cleaned your classroom on this occasion. From now on you will do that yourselves. Four girls will be chosen as class workers which means they will be exempt from dormitory cleaning.'

Bukky raised her hands immediately. 'Excuse me, Ma. Please, I beg of you, can I be a class worker?' She got out of her seat and clasped her hands together desperately. There was a chorus of laughter.

Mrs Folawiyo shot Bukky a look.

'Sorry, Ma, but I am an excellent cleaner of louvres. Ask Flanky, I mean Francesca Davies.'

'That's enough, Miss . . . What is your name?'

'Bukky Adeyemi, Ma. I'm sorry, Ma.' She made a zipped sign across her lips and the class laughed again.

Mrs Folawiyo shook her head. 'As I was saying, I am looking forward to being your class teacher. I hope you will try your best in all parts of the school, not just your studies.'

'Excuse me, Ma!' A girl from the back stood up. She was dressed in white trousers, a white top and a black hijab.

'I am Rashidat, Ma!' She was rushing her words. 'When can we see Shine-Shine River?' As soon as the words left her lips, the class erupted in gasps and squeals.

'Ah well, it is special, isn't it?' Mrs Folawiyo

smiled. 'It is right behind the classroom blocks, you know.'

Every single girl turned round to face the blank wall at the back of the classroom.

'You can't see it unless you climb down the Sandy Hills. Perhaps you will be allowed to go at the weekend after inspection, but swimming in the river is completely forbidden.'

Someone from the back whispered, 'Baba Green will catch anyone who disobeys!'

'And turn them into crocodiles!' Rashidat added, clapping her hands together. This time the gasps were much more fervent. I think I contributed to half of the noise. I was excited and scared all at once.

We were deep into Mrs Aliu's maths lesson when Bolaji walked in dressed in her complete school uniform. Her green khaki dress fitted her like a glove. It was as if it had been sewn privately. She didn't acknowledge the teacher and took the desk next to Bukky. Nobody had chosen it because it already had a heart-shaped padlock on it.

'Young lady! Stand up this minute!' Mrs Aliu's

voice pierced through the classroom at a higher pitch than I ever thought possible.

Bolaji stood up reluctantly, feigning confusion and looking around for support. Flanky and I exchanged looks. We were not buying it. I could see everyone's faces of disapproval. Why wasn't she with us for assembly? How had she got her uniform before us? And how did it look so perfect without adjustments? Where had she gone to change?

'I don't know where you are coming from or who you think you are that you can waltz into my classroom without a word of greeting, but let me tell you now that it will not do! You will remain standing and you will follow me to the staffroom afterwards to clean it!'

Whatever had been causing Bolaji's smugness was thrown out of the window.

'But, Ma, I don't do dust,' she protested. 'At home, the maids do all the dusting.'

'Don't worry, there is no dust in the staffroom, only cobwebs and mosquitoes!' Mrs Aliu snapped back.

Whatever restraint we had shown was now

gone. We were all in stitches. Tears rolled down Flanky's cheeks and I clutched my belly in laughter.

Mrs Aliu shot us a look and we fell silent as she left the class with Bolaji in tow.

Rashidat pinched her nose and clutched her chest. 'At home, the maids do all the dusting.'

The whole class erupted again.

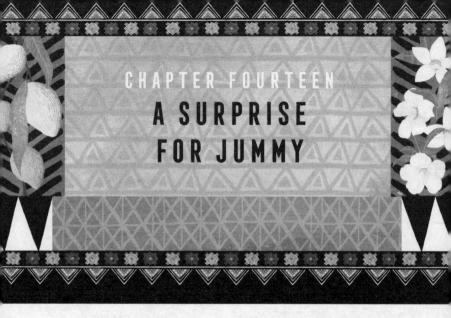

CHAPTER FOURTEEN
A SURPRISE FOR JUMMY

We spent our first day trying to find classrooms and getting very lost in the process. We were all tired and hungry when Alero came into our class to announce that it was time to refit our uniforms. She looked down at us haughtily but smiled warmly at Bolaji. She was going to take us to meet Mrs Folawiyo in front of the home economics lab.

Bolaji stood up and faced us all. 'I've already done mine, Matron's maid did it for me.' She did a twirl in front of the classroom.

Alero smiled. 'Looking good is in our family.'

Flanky shot me and Bukky a look. I shrugged.

The girls who sat by the windows shut the louvres so we could get changed. I looked most ridiculous in my uniform, as did many other girls. Flanky's was too short and Rashidat's green trousers were too long.

'What a nonsense trouser!' She pinched them at the knee and swayed out of the class.

We all walked behind Alero and Bolaji towards the home economics lab. Any time someone tried to get past them, Alero shot them an evil look that sent them back. We were forced to watch them as they sashayed from side to side showing off their well-fitted uniforms.

Finally, we approached the large building that said 'Science and Technology'. A large white van with 'Redbrick Bakery' on the side arrived just as Mrs Folawiyo was coming out of the building. Matron disembarked from it and nodded at our teacher.

'I have brought all the things you will need to fit the girls' dresses.' Matron handed Mrs Folawiyo a white cloth bag.

'Ah, thank you, Matron, what would we do without you at the River School?' Mrs

Folawiyo chirped.

'I have already fitted one of your girls' uniforms. My maid did a superb job. Where is Bolaji?' As soon as she spotted her, she began to smile so widely I thought it would reach her ears. 'Come and show Mrs Folawiyo your dress,' she bellowed.

'And you, come and greet Mrs Folawiyo.' Matron started to speak to someone in the passenger side of the van.

Bolaji was still showing off her uniform when a girl climbed out of the van. There was something familiar about her, about her four braids, her large brown eyes . . . My heart leapt.

'Caro!' I cried out without giving it a second thought.

She looked up and there was a look of horror in her eyes as I ran towards her.

'Afolabi! Get back here!' Mrs Folawiyo called after me, but I couldn't stop myself.

'Caro!' I embraced her.

She was stiff. She didn't hug me back. I looked into her eyes. I saw fear and confusion. She pulled away and adjusted her pinafore dress.

'Jummy, please,' she whispered.

Matron came towards us and shot me the gravest look I ever saw. Caro curtseyed and bent her head very low.

'Young girl, what is your name?' Matron demanded, glaring at me.

'Jumoke Afolabi, Ma! This is Caro! My best friend from home—'

'Well, this is my *maid*!' Matron interrupted me. 'I can assure you, you don't know her. Do you understand me?'

My heart was racing, threatening to burst out of my chest. 'But I do know her!' I insisted.

'Please stop, I am already in enough trouble!' Caro muttered under her breath.

Mrs Folawiyo came closer.

'Matron Armansah, I am so sorry. I don't know what came over this little rascal. She is one of mine.'

'No problem, some of these girls are too tiny to be away from home.' She looked at me with pity.

Mrs Folawiyo led me towards the lab. I was still shaking as I watched Matron and Caro get back into the van and drive off.

I didn't say anything. I couldn't. My mouth had

gone all dry like when you have malaria. My tummy turned and I thought I was going to be sick.

CHAPTER FIFTEEN
THE FIRST RUN

The owl beside my window woke me up once again.

I had woken up almost every hour in what seemed to be the longest night that ever existed. I wanted it to be morning so I could see Caro again. What was she doing here at the River School? How could she be Matron's maid? She had looked so afraid and confused when she saw me.

A terrible thought entered my mind. What if Caro was here against her will? I had heard of gbomo-gbomo, those invisible kidnappers of small children that tainted the seven o'clock news.

An even scarier thought came to hang over my

head as the owl continued to hoot. What if she didn't mind being here? What if she wanted to be a maid? Caro, the great dancer, the great plucker of fruit and winner of ride over, ride over! Impossible! I sat up in my bed, my heart pounding.

I was just about to lie down again when I heard a shout from outside.

'All Nile girls please come out on the lawn before the count of ten!' The voice was familiar. I looked towards Ngozi's bed; it was uncovered and empty.

'One!' Ngozi had started counting.

Gemini jumped down from the top bunk with a thud. I scrambled out of bed. Tope groaned, clutching her tummy, and Bolaji gave a long sigh. Senior Funmi had sent for her last night and she had walked in sulking, but I couldn't care less about her if I tried right now.

Senior Funmi spoke without moving. 'Ngozi will not find it funny if her own room girls are the last out.'

'Eight . . .' Ngozi continued to count. I had almost reached the lawn when Bolaji bent down in front of me to adjust her slippers. I tried to get around her but she just turned the other way so that I couldn't get by. I tried to push past her but she propelled herself quickly on to the lawn just before Ngozi said ten. I on the other hand was just stepping on to the lawn.

Bolaji giggled as Ngozi eyed me coolly.

'All of you that didn't make it, just stand to the right of me. You shall be washing toilets before breakfast!'

Bukky, too, was late. She pinched her nose at me. I managed a smile.

'Listen up all of you! Every weekday will start with a cross-country. A total of five kilometres every morning at 5.30 a.m.'

A groan rippled through the crowd of girls.

'You can grumble all you like but that's the way it is. Nile House will start a new trend of beating every other house this term and acing the Harmattan Games. Is that clear?'

There was a reluctant, 'Yes, Ngozi.'

We went back to our rooms to change into our sportswear. I had never run five kilometres in my life and I didn't think I could do it.

*

I went to look for Bukky when I was ready.

We met Flanky out on the front porch already doing stretches.

'Efiko of sports.' Bukky started to mimic her stretches.

'Efiko of books,' Flanky retorted.

What was I? I wanted to be an efiko of something.

I was still wondering when Ngozi raced out in front of us, blowing her whistle loudly. Flanky followed her instantly along with a host of other zealous girls. Bukky and I jogged slowly, watching the sun rise. It looked beautifully orange as it sat like an egg yolk on the horizon. I wished I could just sit there with Caro and ask her all the questions on my mind.

'Afolabi! Oni!' Ngozi was calling me and Bolaji by our surnames and it sounded like a warning.

'I do not expect anyone in my room to be at the back!' She blew her whistle right in my ear.

'People do not call a royal family name just anyhow,' Bolaji muttered.

I grabbed Bukky's hand and sprinted forwards. I didn't want Ngozi to lump us with Bolaji.

Many girls passed us on the way as Bukky and I jogged slowly, huffing and puffing every so often. I saw the sign for the two-kilometre mark as we jogged past the assembly ground, the hard concrete sending shooting pains through my knees. I was discouraged. How could it be only two kilometres? It felt like we had been running for ever.

We followed the others past the classrooms and huffed up a road that rose up high so that we couldn't see where it ended. It was so hard to climb and my side began to hurt a little. That was where we saw the river. It was so beautiful, flowing quietly under the morning sun. My mouth dropped and Bukky squealed with delight. I wished I could run down the hill and see it up close. Running against the wind coming from the river inspired both of us. We pushed ourselves so that we could see the river from the top. This was a mistake because that little pain in my side became a sharp pain that I could no longer ignore.

I stopped and bent over wheezing, clutching my side in despair.

Bukky came back for me and sat beside me on

the side of the path, patting me on the back, both of us panting heavily.

Ngozi appeared with Bolaji and some other walkers at the back.

'Ngozi, perhaps I should take Jumoke to the sickbay,' Bukky said, still patting me on the back.

'You shall do no such thing. Take a two-minute break and meet me at the dining hall, which is the five-kilometre mark.'

I was shocked. I held my side more dramatically. It really did hurt.

'Save it for someone who cares. I know a lazy lot when I see them. I've seen the dust you've been piling under the lockers!'

My mouth dropped. How did she know?

Bolaji chuckled.

'Yes! You and Madam Bolaji are both very spoilt indeed!'

Bolaji walked off coolly, totally unmoved.

I was not unmoved. I was both embarrassed and livid at the same time! I thought about Chigozie drawing my map for me and Caro writing my lines. Though the pain I was feeling was very real, I jumped to my feet, still pressing my side. It still hurt, but I didn't look back. I didn't wait for Bukky. I just ran.

I kept to the path and ran past the entrance to the staff quarters, which was the three-kilometre mark. I could see Flanky in the distance as I approached the entrance to Princey's cottage, the four-kilometre mark. The pain had subsided now and the feeling of running was exhilarating. What if I could actually run past her? I imagined myself as Mary Onyali for the second time in as many days.

One more kilometre to go. It was then I felt the stabbing sensation again, deeper and more painful than before. I clutched my side again, grimacing and hoping that it would stop somehow. This had never happened to me before, but then I had never had to run for anything. We had run a few metres in primary school but that was easy. I sat down again by the side of the pathway as others raced past.

I was distraught. I had tried so hard. I tried to hold back the tears but I couldn't. They just kept flowing.

Someone came and sat beside me. It was Ngozi. 'So you are not faking it?'

'No', I said in utter defeat. 'I don't think running is for me.'

'Don't count yourself out yet. You must go to the matron today to check yourself out. Just in case!'

I nodded submissively.

She lifted me to my feet gently and put my arm around her. 'Let's walk the rest.'

We walked the last kilometre together in silence.

I was surprised by her kindness and embarrassed that I couldn't finish. Even Bolaji had finished. She came towards me with Bukky and Gemini.

'Hey, Jumoke, are you the only room-one girl that was unable to finish? Maybe it's because you've been mixing with the help around here. This is the River School, you know, not some rubbish school for underachievers—'

I gasped at her meanness.

'Listen, girl,' Gemini broke in, 'shut up before I pulverize you.'

Bolaji laughed and was about to say something, but Ngozi shot her a deadly look and then

116

addressed everyone.

'Well done, girls, for completing the run. If you want to run an extra hundred metres, meet me at the bottom of the dining hall. The fruit tree at the top is a hundred metres from there, OK? You're all welcome to watch.'

She looked at me. 'Afolabi, you are excused.'

Bolaji patted my head and I flinched.

Flanky came up and gave me and Bukky high fives before joining the others for the hundred-metre sprint.

Ngozi blew her whistle and all the runners shot forwards towards the fruit tree. The rest of us started screaming their names.

'Flanky! Flanky!' Bukky and I screamed at the top of our voices. I could still feel a dull ache at my side.

Flanky's arms and legs were in synch. She looked exactly like Mary Onyali, her long body effortlessly passing every other girl. Everyone was now screaming her name.

'Flanky! Flanky!'

I was so proud to know her.

She was just about to reach the fruit tree when

Bolaji appeared as if by magic and propelled herself forwards, puffing her chest out. Ngozi blew her whistle and declared a draw to Bolaji and Flanky. I couldn't believe it. Where had she come from? I was sure I hadn't seen her at the start. Had she cheated?

Nobody seemed to care because the chants changed immediately.

'Flanky! Oni! Flanky! Oni! Nile House superstars!' the girls roared.

'Flanky and Oni, you've got some speed on you! You will do Nile House proud!' Ngozi was shouting above the crowd.

Bukky and I went up to Flanky and put our arms around her. I managed a smile at Bolaji. There was a twinkle in her eye. She leant in and whispered to us, pointing both her thumbs towards herself.

'Too bad I'll soon be in the winning house, Limpopo!'

With that, Bolaji slithered away from the crowd, leaving the three of us staring after her in shock.

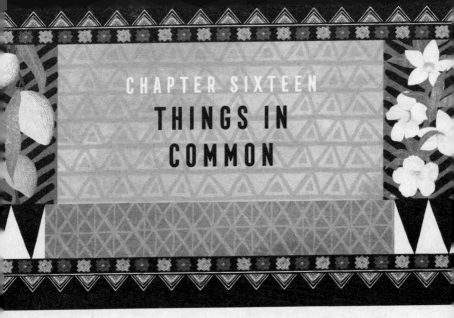

CHAPTER SIXTEEN

THINGS IN COMMON

Bukky and I approached the prefects' toilet with trepidation. This was our punishment for not getting to the lawn on time. I thought I would be exempt because of my side pain, but Ngozi had given me the key straight after the morning run. Bukky and I walked to the end of the row of cubicles, avoiding suspicious-looking puddles of water and pinching our noses to keep out the stench.

I took out the key and unlocked the door. I pushed it and stepped back, afraid of what I would find behind it. Bukky put her T-shirt over her nose. I gasped in horror. I had never seen anything like it in all my life. Liquid started to form in my mouth. Bukky had a peek. We both looked at each other and ran out. We stood in the corridor to my room watching everyone getting ready for the day.

'What are we going to do?' Bukky asked. 'We could start with the floor, maybe remove all the tissue or perhaps try to flush the toilet but there was no water in the . . .'

I was no longer listening. I watched as Senior Moradeke made her way out of the dorm, stopping on the front porch to put up a poster. Bukky was still talking.

'I have a scrubbing brush, not a very strong one but it—'

'Bukky! Bukky!' I shook her shoulders until she came out of her mad cleaning trance. 'I have an idea!'

I mean, I didn't want to be lazy but that toilet belonged to the devil.

I ran into my room and got out my art supplies from my locker. White paper, sticky tape, black marker, red marker. I quickly scribbled on the paper then ran back out and dragged Bukky back to the toilet of death.

'I haven't got any cleaning stuff,' Bukky was shouting as I dragged her along.

We pinched our noses again and walked inside. I pasted my freshly made poster on the prefects' toilet door and locked it firmly.

OUT OF BOUNDS – OPEN AT YOUR OWN RISK!

I had written it in alternating black and red block letters.

Bukky gasped. 'It's genius!' she cried as we gave each other a high five.

By the time Bukky and I entered the dining hall for breakfast, the Nile House area of the hall was rife with excitement. Everyone was talking about how Ngozi was already looking good for the Harmattan Games.

As we walked towards the large metal flasks to queue for tea, someone shouted out, 'N-Squared for Nile House!' Another bunch of senior girls responded with a cry, 'Hey hey hey!'

Ngozi beamed at them and started giving high fives all round. I had never seen her so happy. She looked immaculate in her white shirt and green skirt but she still had on white plimsolls, not brown sandals like the rest of us. Her six large twists sat like a crown on top of her head.

Some juniors and senior girls came up to Flanky to congratulate her.

'Francesca Davies, I hear you were almost as fast as Ngozi,' one senior said.

Bolaji was in front of us in the queue when Alero grabbed her mug and got tea for her. She looked back at us and winked smugly. By the time I got to the table with my tea, she was serving eggs with a scowl on her face while Gemini was serving the bread. I used my side-eye to sneak a peek into the pot. The eggs were scrambled and in fat juicy clumps swimming in watery oil. I was ravenous.

'I hear the Form One girls really shone out there on the field today.' Senior Funmi was looking up and sipping her tea.

'Well, not all of us were able to finish, ehn, Jumoke?' Bolaji smirked as she placed only a tiny ball of scrambled egg on the plate directly in front of me, then dished out huge clumps of eggs for everyone else.

'I heard about your side pain.' Tope spoke for

the first time. 'You better check it out. I heard of this girl who had the same type of thing, turned out to be appendicitis and—'

'Thank you, Tope Lawanson!' Ngozi interrupted. 'Please let's eat without one of your horror health stories. Jumoke, just make sure you go and see Matron Armansah.'

'Matron Armansah is a witch!' Tope declared.

I looked up, worried. So did Bolaji. That did not seem to stop Tope.

'It's true, she only cares about rich girls. One time, she gave my friend penicillin without checking if she was allergic!'

'That's enough, Tope!' both Ngozi and Senior Funmi demanded.

'Matron is not bad,' Gemini added for my benefit.

'If you were on scholarship like me, you would know the real Matron!'

'Ahem!' Senior Funmi gave Tope a look that silenced all of us.

Bolaji smiled.

I took the measly plate of eggs in front of me and looked at the one Bolaji had taken. It had a mound of juicy scrambled eggs on it. My eyes met hers and she stared back coldly. She was just about to start eating.

'Bolaji, swap plates with Jumoke, thank you very much.' Ngozi's eyes met Bolaji's.

She opened her mouth to protest but Ngozi just made the swap herself.

'There should be no problem with that, Bolaji, because I'm sure you served everyone equally, didn't you?' A smile was dancing on Ngozi's lips.

'She's got you there.' Gemini was laughing and really enjoying herself.

I was a bit worried about the really angry look on Bolaji's face. She looked like she would push me into a ditch the first chance she got. Between her anger and the witch of a matron, I was petrified.

I left the dining hall with Gemini, armed with many questions.

'What happened to the girl who was allergic to penicillin?'

'Don't let Tope into your head, she is obsessed with illnesses. She's here on a theatre scholarship, you know. A brilliant profession for all her drama, for sure.'

I smiled for a mini second. 'Yes, but what happened to that girl, where is she now?'

'I don't even know where Tope got that story from. Her paranoia knows no bounds. Honestly, it's probably all made up for dramatic effect!'

'I don't want to go to the matron any more,' I declared, ignoring Gemini's attempts to allay my fears.

'I'll go with you if you like. I mean Matron is not the coolest but she's all right. We can go at first break.'

I was really pleased with that. 'Thanks, Gemini, that means a lot.'

'That's what roomies are for.' We walked up the narrow path that led to the assembly ground, surrounded by thick bushes and trees on either side. There were many girls ahead of us and I looked back to see how many were behind us. I nearly jumped out of my oversized uniform as a girl bumped into me. It was Bolaji. She was right there in my face, her cold eyes looking into mine.

'Bolaji, how long have you been behind us?' I said, pulling away from her.

Gemini came between us. 'If you're looking for

friends, I can tell you now, we ain't it!'

Bolaji looked at me. 'So you don't want to be my friend, Jumoke?'

I wanted to belt out, 'Not really!' but it seemed wicked. 'Well, you don't seem as if you want to be friends, Bolaji,' I said carefully.

'Maybe I do!' She beamed at me and it was creepy.

I looked at Gemini.

'Suit yourself, Jummy.' Gemini shrugged. 'I know a slimeball when I see one. Bolaji, stay away from me or I'll use your skinny legs to make spaghetti.'

I laughed as she ran off, but Bolaji was scowling. 'Gemini is just being Gemini,' I said, trying to make peace. 'She is really cool.'

'My father would not let me be friends with such a girl. She is so common. But I suppose you don't mind having those sorts of friends.' She looked straight into my eyes and I knew she was talking about Caro.

'What do you want from me, Bolaji?'

'I actually think you and I have a lot in common. You just seem to like a certain type of—'

'We don't have anything in common, Bolaji! You are mean for no reason and you think you are better than everyone else.'

'Well, it's true. I come from a royal family who own the largest bakery in the country. My grandfather is a king and of his sixty grandchildren, I am sure I'm his favourite.'

'Seriously, Bolaji, just stop. Nobody wants to know.'

'Limpopo girls want to know. When I go there to see my cousin, they all crowd round me like desperate little puppies. It's fascinating really.' She was smiling her sly smile like when she'd served me a tiny ball of egg earlier.

There was now a twinkle in her eye. I looked at her uniform, all starched, ironed and hugging her body like a glove. I looked down at mine. I hadn't had time to get Mrs Folawiyo to adjust it for me. It hung on me like a sack of rice.

'You know who made my dress look so smart? Your friend, the girl at Matron's. My very own maid!' She wielded those words like a knife.

'Caro is *your* maid?' I threw all composure out of the window. 'You are a very spoilt girl!'

'See? We do have lots in common.' She smirked. 'You don't like work either – like sweeping or completing races.' This time she threw me an evil wink. 'I couldn't possibly wash my own clothes and bed sheets. How ridiculous would that be?' She rolled her eyes. 'And as for morning duties, my grandfather is making sure I am moved to Limpopo before the first dorm inspections . . .'

She went on and on. I stood there in shock.

'. . . Did you know that Limpopo have won the last five Harmattan Games? As for Nile House, well you heard what Princey said.'

Suddenly, something rose up in me. I wanted to be part of making sure Nile House won the games for the first time. I was not going to ask anyone to do work for me – I was determined not to be like Bolaji.

'Well! We are not going to let that happen. *I* am not going to let that happen!' I said, beating my chest with so much might I started to cough.

Bolaji pulled a face. 'Well you'll have to sort your frail self out first, won't you? First you had a side pain and now you are coughing. Let's see if you are fit enough to run half a kilometre.' She patted my back and I shrugged her off.

'Look here, Bolaji, you think I don't know that you cheated in that race with Flanky . . .' Just then, the bell for assembly started to ring.

'Aha! Saved by the bell. Got to run – unlike some who can't.' She wasn't running, she was actually skipping in the air like a springbok.

I was so vexed I wished I had a pebble to throw at her.

For days I avoided going to Matron. Ngozi did not allow me to run at all. Every morning, I'd hear of yet another girl who had shone at running. I wanted to shine too.

Then at assembly one day, Princey announced that try-outs for the Harmattan Games would take place after first break for those who were interested. What if this pain of mine really turned out to be appendicitis like Tope said? I had never felt anything like it even when Caro and I played 'police and thief' with ThankGod and Owolabi, who were always the police giving us a ferocious chase round the compound.

I made up my mind to go to Matron on my own, before the try-outs. I wanted to be part of a winning Nile House and for that I needed to be fit!

At first-break bell, I took the path past the assembly ground and through the tall trees surrounding Princey's cottage. The cottage was even prettier at the back with an excellent array of flowers, some in the ground and others in colourful ceramic plant pots. There were butterflies making their home in this haven and laundry hung on the clothes line: adire, tie-dye, ankara in different styles and colours.

Just as the sickbay cottage came into view, I saw a lanky figure standing in front of an array of brilliant bougainvillea. He held a large pair of garden shears and was attempting to prune the purple bush. I recognized him from the school gate. He was wearing dark overalls and not a green kaftan as promised by the girls, but he did look very scary as he wielded his garden shears trying to cut a very thick branch. I wondered how to walk past him. I decided to just go for it.

'Good morning, sir!' I muttered as I walked

past him with my heart racing and my eyes fixed to the ground as if I was looking for something there. He mumbled something and I kept on walking towards the sickbay that stood just a few metres ahead. Matron's white Redbrick van was parked outside. I began to feel wary. Would Matron tell me off for carrying on when I saw Caro? I walked up the short steps to the cottage in trepidation.

I could hear the swish of a broom. The sweeper stopped as they heard me approach. It was Caro sweeping the corridor of the cottage. My heart began to thump again but this time I held myself back and only whispered her name. She looked up at me with her big brown eyes. They were filled with sadness and my heart went out to her.

'Jummy!'

'Caro, what are you doing here?' I continued to whisper.

'We cannot talk now.'

'Are you always with Matron?'

Caro bit her lip. She was about to say something when Matron squealed with delight from one of the rooms inside.

Caro jumped and returned to her sweeping.

Matron appeared.

'You are always welcome in my office, you hear?' She moved to the side to let the other person out.

It was Bolaji. In her hands was a pack of purple-checked cloth.

'Ah, Jumoke, look at my Limpopo housewear,' she said, when she saw me. 'I shall be going to my beloved Limpopo at last!'

As she walked off, she bumped into Caro sweeping and dropped the purple cloth she was holding. I could swear she had done it deliberately.

'Look how you have dirtied my new dresses. How careless!' Bolaji turned to Matron.

'Caro, please stop that sweeping at once!' Matron yelled. 'Can't you see Bolaji is trying to get by? And you have a lot of washing and ironing to do too!'

'Ah yes, I will send my uniform for washing.' Bolaji flashed a mean smile. 'Oh and my hair needs redoing.' She picked up one of her plaits and let it fall over her forehead.

Caro nodded and put her broom behind her

back, her eyes to the floor.

Bolaji raised one of her eyebrows haughtily at Caro.

She looked her up and down and walked off with an exaggerated air of disgust.

My heart wanted to jump out of my chest. I wanted to fight for Caro but I knew that it would make things worse, not better.

'Small girl, come in. I remember you.' Matron ushered me into her office.

I heard the sound of a bell in the distance. Not only had I missed try-outs but Bolaji had made a mockery of my best friend! Gemini was right. She was a slimeball and a spoilt little brat!

To make matters worse, Matron told me off for wasting her time. She said my pain was only a stitch!

I felt stupid, angry and deflated all at once.

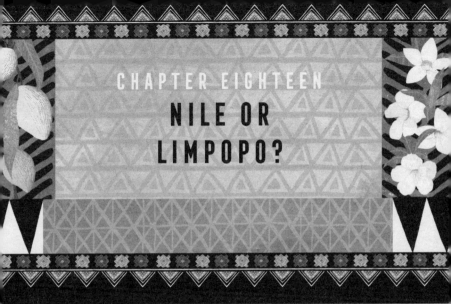

CHAPTER EIGHTEEN

NILE OR LIMPOPO?

Ever since I first saw Caro here, I had been waking up before the first bell, my emotions all over the place. I could not enjoy all that was the River School, knowing my best friend was not happy here. And then there was Bolaji. I looked at her empty bed. Was she with her cousin again or busy getting Caro to do all her dirty work at Matron's?

I looked at my watch glowing in the dark. It was just after 6 a.m. Usually, I would hear the owl outside our room. I had tried once to see him through the windows but it would mean peering behind Ngozi's bed. I imagined him to be perching on the large tree that stood outside Nile House. This morning, the sounds were different. I could hear slippers slapping along the corridors, buckets being dragged from underneath beds and the sounds of brooms splashing against water and concrete. It was easier to imagine the owl.

Senior Moradeke's voice broke my thoughts as she screamed for Form One to Four girls to come out to the lawn. I was so used to Ngozi's authoritative voice demanding our presence for the morning run that I felt uncompelled to obey Senior Moradeke despite her large size.

'Before the count of ten. One . . .'

Everyone rushed out of their beds. Even Tope hurried too without any ailment troubling her, yet. Gemini jumped down straight into her slippers, nearly knocking my head off in the process. 'You better not be the last, Jumoke. The punishment will be to wash extra toilets!'

That got me going. I flew into my slippers and joined the others on the lawn.

'Today is the first Saturday of term,' Senior Moradeke began, 'which means the first Inspection. For the JJCs amongst us, Mrs Aliu, our housemistress, Princey and Matron Armansah will be visiting our dorms at noon – Nile House is usually first to be inspected. Points will be given to the cleanest house. Each house also wins points for sports, good behaviour and exceptional work in lessons. At the end of the term, the house with the most points gets to have a picnic on Princey's lawn. Nile House has not had that opportunity since I started in this school and I can see why.'

She gave us a most serious stare.

'For example, someone put an "out of bounds" poster on the prefects' toilet instead of cleaning it!'

My heart began to beat ferociously. I looked over at Bukky who looked back at me with the same fear in her eyes.

'Now that morning duties have been properly assigned, I hope that will not happen again!'

I could feel Ngozi's eyes boring into me. I didn't look at her.

Senior Moradeke continued. 'I hear N-Squared, I mean Ngozi Nwobi, is on the verge of making this happen with the Nile House track team. Let's not spoil her hard work. Before breakfast, make sure you have prepped your various duty areas for scrubbing. If you are a class worker, your class will be inspected too and the cleanest class will get points for their respective houses.

'If you impress the inspectors,' she went on, 'perhaps you can all have a fun day at' – she paused – 'Shine-Shine River.' She said it in an exaggerated whisper.

There was a loud cheer. Even Ngozi looked excited.

'Now go and prep your areas of work!'

We all scampered off the lawn in eager anticipation.

I caught up with Gemini.

'So how do I prep the room for cleaning?'

'Girl, your job is the easiest. All you have to do is clear under the beds, take everything to the box room and get your cleaning equipment ready. Then make sure you sweep the room floor just like you have done every morning. After breakfast, you will mop and dust and stuff, right?'

'Sounds easy enough!' I said. This time I was determined to do a proper job.

When we got back to our room, we walked

right into an argument between Senior Funmi, Ngozi and Alero, who had come with two dutiful-looking Limpopo girls.

'Look, just tell me where all her things are and let me go,' Alero was saying. 'You girls have bullied Bolaji enough.' She shot me a look as I tried to get to my bunk. 'If it isn't Ngozi's little spoilt brat!'

My mouth dropped. 'I'm not the one who is—'

Ngozi interrupted. 'Don't fall into Alero's trap, Jumoke, she is just waiting for you to say something so she can punish you.'

'Look! It is against the rules to just move houses without permission,' Senior Funmi said with her arms crossed.

'I have permission! Bolaji's dad is not only the CEO of Redbrick Bakery but also a patron of this school and he demanded by telephone yesterday that Bolaji be moved. She already has her new Limpopo housewear. I don't want to wait till after inspection to move. You know Limpopo takes inspection seriously.'

As she said this, she looked disapprovingly around our room. She scrunched up her nose and dragged her fingers along the top of a locker. It was covered in dust.

'You mean you don't want Bolaji to do any scrubbing!' Ngozi's voice was getting louder.

'Just let her go. It's Bolaji's loss not ours!' Senior Funmi said.

Alero sucked her teeth and faced me.

'Jumoke Afolabi! Go and show these girls where Bolaji's suitcase is. Gemini, put all Bolaji's bath things in her bucket over there. Don't bother with the cleaning stuff, she won't be needing it!' With that, she stormed out and slammed the door behind her.

The room was quiet for about a second, then Gemini walked to the door in exactly the same manner as Alero had done but shaking her back-side vigorously. All five of us burst into fits of laughter. The Limpopo girls did not laugh. I took them to the box room and showed them Bolaji's things, which were clearly marked in silver ink. Everyone else's was in black ink.

When I returned, everyone was hard at work, dusting, sweeping and clearing underneath the beds. I creased my brows dramatically so that

Senior Funmi saw that I disagreed with them doing my work. I didn't want to be anything like Bolaji who didn't do her own jobs.

Senior Funmi looked at me and smiled. 'I have spoken to Senior Moradeke and we have decided to come together to clean the room, while you and Gemini will do the sink area which was supposed to be Bolaji's work.'

I couldn't believe Bolaji was getting away with not doing her share but I was happy that we would all be pulling together.

I smiled back. 'That is a splendid idea, Senior Funmi.'

I followed Gemini to the sink area where we found Flanky shaking her head in despair.

She looked up when she saw us. 'Where is your silly room-mate Bolaji? I cannot do my morning duty until she cleans those.' She pointed to the two large ceramic sinks, which were full of orange stagnant water. It turned my stomach just looking at it and it smelt bad.

I started to think I should have saved my 'out of bounds' poster for this.

'Have no fear, room-one girls are here.' Gemini

lifted her bucket in the air. When she put it down, I saw a sink plunger, several rags and torn pieces of foam from old mattresses. I was surprised by her enthusiasm.

She sensed my confusion. 'I'll do anything to not be outdone by those Limpopo bullies. Let this be the year that Nile House knocks Limpopo off its high horse.'

I was pumped by Gemini's speech. 'Yes, go Nile House girls! We are the best!' I grabbed one of the rags from her bucket and slapped it on my lap. This set Flanky off in high spirits.

'I knew I would be lucky today.'

I rolled my eyes.

'Well, there's no wood around here is there?' Flanky winked cheekily.

'Come on, girls, let's do this!' Gemini put her entire arm into the orange water in one of the sinks and started bringing out all of the things inside. She looked at me. 'Well don't just stand there. Get in!'

I looked at Flanky.

'Don't look at me, I'm doing this after you're done.' She was now pointing to the floor below the sinks, which was wet and grimy too.

I put my hand just above the surface of the water in the second sink. Gemini pushed my hand in. It was disgusting to say the least. There were a few plates and some cutlery at the bottom, but mostly it was little pieces of bathing soap, leftover food and gooey gunk. I shrieked as I yanked my arm out. I looked at the orangeness of the grime and looked down at the orangeness of my housewear.

'OK, then! Nile House, this is for you!' Nobody could stop me now. I plunged deep into the sink. I had never even washed the clean toilets at home but now here I was, hands deep in the worst mess I'd ever seen. It was all our mess and I was proud to be part of cleaning it up.

Suddenly, as Gemini stirred the orange gloop in the sink, she began to sing.

'One fine day, Mama cook soup!' She sang it really loudly and started to look through the brick that separated the sink area from the lawn. There was an immediate response.

'Ogbono soup aye!'

She continued, 'Salt no dey, pepper no dey.'

'Ogbono soup aye!' they bellowed back. I

could see through the perforated brick wall that Lola and Tayo were amongst the singers.

I laughed and continued to drop the things I found in the sink into my bucket. I got it now. Gemini was pretending to be the cook of a terrible pot of ogbono soup. I had eaten it once in Owolabi's house. It looked like slime, just like okro soup, but was very delicious. It looked a little like the gloop that we were stirring in the sink. Gemini went louder still.

'Onion no dey, stock no dey.'

'Ogbono soup aye,' came the insistent reply.

She went through my mother's entire condiment cabinet, insisting this wretched soup was without any useful ingredients until there was a loud cry from the lawn. 'Cook, no cook me nonsense!'

There was a loud cheer and then we carried on with our work. We used big bowls to pour the slimy orange water into old buckets and then emptied it into the gutters that surrounded the lawn. Finally, we got out the plungers and sucked out the last of the mess. Flanky, Gemini and I raised a merry cheer when we heard the throat of the sink burp it away. Gemini turned on the tap and we rejoiced as the water went freely down the drains.

Flanky was smiling and humming a tune happily as she too got on with cleaning the floor.

The breakfast bell rang and I looked at my watch. How would we get clean in time for breakfast?

Gemini laughed. 'Breakfast is coming to us today. Mama Tea and the other kitchen women will come to each cottage with trolleys of fresh bread and canisters of tea! Let's get washed and ready.'

I was intrigued.

'Mama Tea must make extra-special tea!'

'You got that right!' Gemini confirmed it.

It seemed that though Inspection Saturday was hard work, it was also so much fun indeed.

There was a long queue for the showers, which were clean for a change, and I didn't have to bath beside the lawn in broad daylight. The bathrooms smelt of strong disinfectant and I rushed my shower and dressed quickly. Nile House were usually served first and I wanted to be there when the trolleys arrived.

CHAPTER NINETEEN

FIRST INSPECTION

Mama Tea and the other kitchen ladies looked really up to the task in their royal-blue aprons and hairnets. They pushed the trolleys which carried Redbrick loaves of bread and a big metal bowl with a large heap of boiled eggs. There was a large flask and big tubs of butter. It looked so delicious and I wasn't the only one that thought so. Tope's stomach growled.

Gemini looked at her and laughed. 'Grubido!'

'Room one, six girls,' Tope said when we got to the trolley.

I was about to object and say we were now five but she shot me a look.

The kitchen woman grabbed three loaves of bread and six eggs and gave them to Tope. Gemini put forward a plate and large jug which was filled with piping-hot ready-made tea, complete with milk and, I hoped, sugar. The butter was golden yellow and melting in the morning heat.

We shared the meal sitting on buckets turned upside down around Ngozi's bed. It was such a lovely morning and I felt really close to everyone. The way we had come together today made me feel like part of a really great team. I was glad I hadn't shied away from emptying the sink. It was disgusting but it felt good being there for each other like that.

We were standing to attention by our beds, waiting for the inspectors to arrive, when Tope looked out of the window and sighed.

'I hoped Matron Armansah wouldn't be there. She is so unfair.' Her voice suddenly changed as she mimicked the matron. 'My heart bleeds for girls like you.'

We were still laughing when the inspectors knocked on our door.

Senior Funmi walked over and opened it, curtseying as she said good afternoon.

I recognized everyone. Following Senior Moradeke was our housemistress, Mrs Aliu, in a black scarf and kaftan. Princey was next, looking as sharp as ever in a bright blue kaftan and blue slippers with green feathers on them. Her head tie today was a simple blue scarf, loose at the back. She was followed by Matron Armansah in her crisp white dress with blue hat and white shoes.

'Good afternoon,' we all chorused.

'Good afternoon,' they replied, Mrs Aliu's voice piercing through my chest.

They started peering at our beds and slipping their hands into different corners of our room. They were smiling and nodding their heads. Matron Armansah turned to Tope.

'Tope, I have not seen you in my clinic this term. Miracles shall never cease.' Tope made a petrified and awkward face as they turned away. There was a murmur of giggles.

'The real miracle is how clean Nile House is this term.' Princey was smiling, obviously impressed with the state of our room. This made Mrs Aliu squeal in delight.

'Miss Miller, not up to mischief yet this term?' Princey said, looking at Gemini.

'Not at all, Ma.' She beamed, trying to look angelic.

Suddenly, Mrs Aliu frowned as she saw the unlaid bed. 'Why is this bed empty?'

Senior Funmi stepped forward.

'Ma, it belonged to Bolaji Oni, a cousin to Alero Oni who came to take her stuff away today, saying that—'

Matron interrupted. 'Ah, I remember now. Bolaji's dad phoned to say she had been really ill several times and so she may do better with her older cousin. Do you remember, Ma?'

Princey nodded in pensive agreement.

'But Ma, she was never ill here. She was always with her cousin.' Senior Funmi was evidently upset.

Matron raised her eyebrows and peered down at us as if she had some imaginary glasses. 'Bolaji was at my clinic the other day! A real gem of a girl. I gave her an exemption from morning duties. She has a bad back, you know. Poor girl.'

'Well, if Matron says she has to move then so be it. It looks like this room is perfect as it is.' Princey swiped her hand over a locker and smiled.

'If all the rooms are like this, Nile House will do well this term,' Mrs Aliu added proudly.

Princey looked at Matron. 'I think the girls deserve a treat from the tuck shop today, don't you?'

Matron shot me a look. 'Well, it depends on what the other rooms look like.'

Princey cut in. 'Well just on the basis of this room alone, I am convinced.'

'OK, Ma, I went to the bakery today. The van is full to the brim with delicious treats. I've parked just by the river.'

'Brilliant! You all deserve a fun day by Shine-Shine River.'

'Oh Princey!' I cried, unable to stop myself. Everyone gasped as I covered my mouth with my hand.

'I know you call me Princey instead of Principal! As long as you don't start calling Matron

"Matey", we'll be all right.' Princey winked.

We all giggled but Matron's face was as hard as a rock.

'Now remember! No swimming in the river!' Princey added.

Everyone was beaming with excitement as the inspectors left our room, and Senior Funmi could not help giving us all individual high fives.

I loved being in Nile House, room one. Now that Bolaji had left, it was perfect, just perfect!

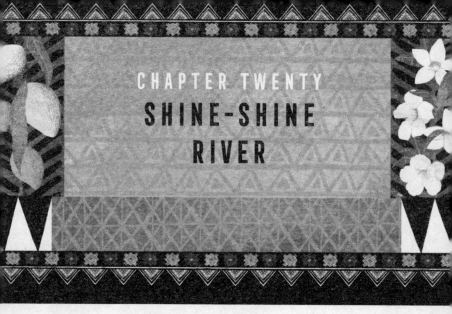

CHAPTER TWENTY
SHINE-SHINE RIVER

Since Nile House was the first to be inspected, we were the very first to head out towards the river. I was so excited. Flanky had come to my room straight after inspection and Lola, Tayo and Michelle had come to get Gemini. Bukky was in class with the other class workers waiting to be inspected.

We had all changed into our orange games shorts and River School white sports tops. Gemini wore a large sun hat and had a long, thick rope and a hoop on her shoulder. Lola had a bag full of sweets and a deck of cards, Michelle had some board games and Tayo had a notepad and several pens. Flanky and I had been lumbered with the blankets, cups and plates.

'We have just under an hour with Shine-Shine all to ourselves. The other houses will start trickling in soon.' Tayo was already writing in her notepad.

'Why is it called Shine-Shine River?' I asked.

'You'll soon see for yourself,' she responded.

'I think I can smell the snacks already,' Michelle declared.

We hurried past the classrooms at record speed, crossed a tarred road and then ran across a large expanse of green. When we came to the end of the green, my mouth dropped. I looked at Flanky, her short black bob bouncing in the wind. She was as awestruck as I was.

Below us lay a valley of dry red soil surrounded by red mounds of sandy hills. It was like God had dipped his hand into the ground and taken a chunk out just to make the river stand out. Though there was a brown wire fence surrounding most of it, Shine-Shine River lay before us glistening in all its glory. There were large trees that had swings and hammocks attached to some of their branches. There were also benches and fallen tree trunks for sitting. This was the perfect playground.

'Does it always shine like that?' I whispered.

'Always!' Lola answered in a whisper too.

'Are we ever allowed to go into the river?' Flanky asked.

'See that shuttle van over there?' Lola pointed to a van parked where the brown wire fence ended, the only point where you could actually get into the river. 'That means Baba Green is about. You won't see him unless there's a problem.'

'Like a crocodile?' I dared to ask.

'Mhm! And sometimes when he gets bored, he turns troublesome girls into them!' Gemini snapped her fingers for effect.

'Look!' Michelle shouted. 'A more important van.' It was the Redbrick Bakery one.

Lola shrieked, 'One, two, three, let's go!'

The Form Two girls held hands and ran down the hill, screaming and laughing as they went down. Flanky looked at me, and we did the same. The wind drew water from my eyes and I squealed in delight as we made our descent towards the van.

It was the one I had seen Caro and Matron in. I ran towards it, letting go of Flanky's hand, hoping desperately that my friend was in it. Matron would not be here for another three hours according to Tayo. The others were still running quite fast but I managed to speed past even Flanky and get to the van first. There was no one in the front. I went round to the back and saw the double doors wide open. Inside were shelves loaded from top to bottom with Redbrick Bakery sticky buns, puffpuff, chinchin, sweets and drinks. There was a calculator and a notepad on the wooden table that separated the inside from the outside of the van.

'Hello?' I called out hopefully.

There was a sudden movement from inside and Caro lifted her head from below a shelf.

'Caro!' My heart leapt with joy.

'Jumoke!' Caro said quietly, a worried look on her face as she looked out behind me.

'Matron is not here,' I reassured her but she still looked anxious. 'She will not finish inspecting for another three hours.'

The other girls had now joined us.

'Tayo, tell her!' I said.

Even though Tayo was confused, she couldn't help herself.

'Yes, I can confirm, Matron will not be here for another two hours and fifty minutes!'

Caro unlocked the wooden gate connected to the wooden table and jumped out. I hugged her tight and this time she hugged me back.

I turned to face the other girls.

'This is my best friend in the whole wide world. Her name is Caro and she is good at everything!'

Gemini introduced everyone.

'You have so much to tell me, Caro!' I said at last.

'Yes, but Matron put me here to sell all these things by the time she comes back.' Caro held out her hands towards the inside of the truck.

'Michelle and I are pretty good with numbers,' said Tayo. 'We would love to be in charge of the shop while you girls catch up.'

Caro bit her lip. 'How will we know when Matron arrives?'

'Limpopo will be last to be inspected,' Michelle said, 'so once we see the girls in purple we'll know dorm inspections are over. Then the inspectors have to make it down for the classroom checks and that gives us another hour after that.'

'Spoken like a true efiko of information!' Tayo said proudly.

Other Nile House girls started to arrive at the truck. Caro jumped back on and started to sell. Tayo and Michelle paid close attention.

A line formed. Gemini ordered first.

'Two honey loaves, five sticky buns, two packets of chinchin and fifteen puffpuff.'

'Leave some for the rest of us,' someone shouted from the queue.

Caro went to the shelves, took down Gemini's order and sorted the change out.

'You're very quick,' Tayo said.

'She is brilliant at numbers!' I said proudly.

'Well, so are we. We've got this. Mark my word, there won't be a single sticky bun left when we are done!'

This seemed to give Caro the confidence to leave them to it.

We followed the other girls towards the high wired fence that separated the river from the red soil. Gemini and Lola took their shoes off. Caro and I did the same. A girl ran past us and shouted, 'Be careful the crocodiles don't bite off your feet.'

Caro and I shrank back. Gemini threw her head back and laughed. She shouted to us.

'We don't know if it is true but once when the river overflowed, a crocodile came into the school. After that, the fence went up.'

'Crocodiles can still come from there,' Caro whispered, pointing to where the shuttle van was parked.

'Baba Green is there,' I whispered back.

'Who be dat?' Caro's eyes opened very wide.

'The man at the gate. They say he can make you crawl crawl like crocodile.' I tried to sound as if I understood it myself.

I looked at her and we both shrugged and burst into laughter.

We walked closer to the fence. The red soil became soft at this point and sometimes a little bit of water rushed past the fence and on to our bare feet. Caro and I dug our toes in. I wrapped my fingers around the wired fence and let the water wash my feet.

There was something so soothing and satisfying in watching the river go by with the sun shining directly on it. Wet wind blew against my face and the air smelt fresh, unlike the Lagos lagoon. That smelt like a thousand people had forgotten to flush the toilet. In the distance, I could see many canoes parked on the shore and I imagined Baba Green in one of them. I thought he must be very strong to ride on top of a crocodile. The thought of that filled me with both admiration and dread.

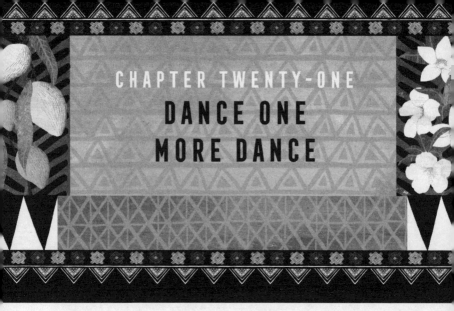

CHAPTER TWENTY-ONE
DANCE ONE MORE DANCE

The river brought me back from my reverie by making swishy-swashy sounds against the big rocks sitting at its edges.

'Matron said I am not to talk to girls like you.' I grinned at Caro.

'Yeah, only ajebutter ones like that one over there.' Caro grinned back, pointing to a girl who was hopping about to avoid the water touching her toes.

We giggled.

Caro's face became serious again.

'You should have seen Matron when she came to our house just before the summer. She was so grand in her crisp white dress and cap. She brought so many things for our family: yams, eggs, corn, bundles of fabric, bread, sticky treats like the ones in the van. She told Mama that all I have to do is clean her house in the morning and then she will send me to nursing school and pay for everything. Everyone was excited except me. I never said I wanted to be a nurse!' Caro made a face. 'If I could be anything' – she paused and looked longingly at the river – 'I'd be a dancer, no a mathematician.' She shrugged and let out a deep sigh. 'Anyway, there was no time for fantasies, Matron said we had to go that evening because of registration and sewing my nurse uniform.'

'I only see you wearing this blue pinafore and working for Matron. Where is your nurse uniform?'

'Ask me o! The last time I raised the topic, she shouted at me for one hour! She used big big words to show her anger.'

'Can't you tell your father to come and pick you up?'

'Jumoke, you always think we are wearing the same slippers.'

I smiled sadly. Caro was so clever with words.

'My parents are really struggling with the seven of us. It was a huge relief to them to have one less mouth to feed. Will I now return because of a few insults? Ingrate! Yes, that was one of the words she called me!'

Caro took her feet out of the water. We walked towards the trees that had swings hanging from them. We chose one that had two swings facing the river.

'I don't understand, though. Why does she need you?' I sat on the swing, my feet not touching the red soil. Caro sat on the other swing, her feet firmly on the ground.

'She needs a maid. Someone to go to the market, cook food, clean the house, wash clothes, plait hair for girls like Princess Bolaji and, as you can see, sell her tasty treats. I even do Bolaji's homework. The maths here is too hard for her.'

'That Bolaji is a spoilt brat,' I snapped. 'So how did she pass the exams?'

Caro shrugged and whispered very low. 'Matron went to Bolaji's house and gave her the questions.'

'What? How do you know this?' I practically screamed.

'Ssh!' This girl! You want to put me in hot soup, ehn? Don't tell anyone because they will know it's me.' The fear I had seen in Caro's eyes that first day started to return. 'Swear you won't tell.'

She wanted me to put my finger on my tongue and raise it to the sky but I couldn't. This was too much. Mama always warned me to never promise to keep a secret when the person themselves had already failed to keep it. *If it is too much for them, then it will be too much for you.*

'Just tell me, Caro. I want to know.' I nudged her shoulder with mine.

She began to speak after a thoughtful pause. 'You remember the time wey I first see you for here?' I smiled inside. Caro only spoke pidgin when she was relaxed.

'Yes!' I said, recalling my astonishment at seeing her here that first time.

'Later that evening, Bolaji and Alero came over to Matron's and even though they tried to whisper, I heard most of what they said. At first, I couldn't understand why Matron was so worked up after seeing you. She told them that the principal must never find out that she had hired a maid for Bolaji. Alero laughed and said that the maid was for her too, otherwise she would tell Princey. Bolaji did not laugh when she told Alero that before she got here Matron did not even know her name. They got into a huge fight and then Alero said that Bolaji was not even supposed to get into the River School if not that Matron had shown her the exam papers beforehand. If you know how loud Matron shouted at them to keep quiet, but they didn't even answer her, they turned on her saying their grandfather helped her get the sole contract to sell Redbrick Bakery snacks. After they left, Matron warned me never to talk to you again. She said she could make things very difficult for my family but I could tell she was really afraid.'

I was speechless – almost. 'That explains a lot. I noticed that straight after the day I saw you, Bolaji was out to get me personally. I don't feel sorry for Matron, they are all birds of the same feather.'

'Hm, I think Matron is more like me than you think. My mother said that Matron was very poor in our village and she became rich just like that, so she can change my life.'

'Your heart is like this river, Caro! You can never be like Matron!' I declared quietly.

Caro laughed.

'You should be in school, Caro! It's your right! Instead, you are here serving girls who don't deserve to be here.'

'Maybe primary school is enough.' Caro sighed yet again.

'But you are brighter than anyone here.' I was getting upset.

'I don't know about that!' Caro looked down at her feet.

I looked at this girl whose grandma had once said she was better than five sons. Caro's grandma was right. She was stronger than all the boys in our compound put together. She could carry two metal buckets full of water without breaking a sweat. She was the very opposite of Bolaji who was a cheat. A cheat at exams and a cheat at running! I thought of the times I had done anything I could to get out of doing my work. Was I a cheat too?

The sound of drumming broke my thoughts

and both Caro and I turned our back on the river to take a look. It was a group of girls in a circle. Tope was one of them. The drummers used jerrycans and empty soda bottles to make music, while the girls in the circle sang and clapped around the girl in the middle who danced her heart out. When the song finished, the dancer in the middle pointed to someone and that girl went into the middle to dance. The song was meaningless but catchy and Caro and I joined the girls, clapping and attempting to sing.

We are the busy little girls.
We are the busy little girls.
We've come to do our shopping
For today's our shopping day
We've got money in our pockets
And a basket full of roses
Some little things we're needing
Just a little tea and sugar
Some bread and poraro
And some pepper and some curry
GBISH!
Poraro!

Flanky whispered loudly, 'What is poraro?'

Lola heard her and shouted back, 'Potato, of course! You ajebutter!'

I laughed until I hurt.

'I'm no butter-eater!' Flanky retorted.

I started to shake my waist vigorously to prove I was not an ajebutter like Flanky. Gemini roared with laughter at the sight of me. The whole atmosphere was buzzing with the beat of our music. Seniors passed by tapping their feet or shaking their waists as they drained soda from their bottles.

Then, to my utmost surprise and delight, the girl in the middle pointed at Caro. Caro looked around her and put her hand to her chest to confirm the selection. The crowd cheered and clapped even harder. She went in. The claps grew louder still and Caro began to dance.

She moved with such grace, her waist swaying enthusiastically to the exact beat. She danced effortlessly with her head down, parallel to her feet, her hands moving as if beating her own imaginary drum. Then she raised her arms above her and took them down again, only this time she dipped her body so low that her pinafore touched the ground.

The crowd roared in delight. And then the song ended: 'Gbish! Poraro!' There was only a heartbeat of silence and then everyone erupted in applause. She thought we were clapping for ourselves so she joined in too.

'They're cheering for you, Caro, for you!' I chimed excitedly.

Her wide brown eyes were glistening with tears.

'You're an excellent dancer, Caro!' cried Gemini.

'Pure class,' Tope added.

'She must not let that talent go to waste.'

I was still smiling from that comment when I saw a group of girls in purple shorts running down the grassy hill towards us. Matron would soon arrive!

'Quick, Caro, inspection will soon be over.'

Caro walked hastily towards the van. Gemini, Lola and I followed.

Tayo and Michelle were counting money and putting it into the cash register. Caro was just making the switch when Bolaji arrived with her cousin and her entourage of Limpopo girls.

Tayo and Michelle jumped down from the van swiftly. Tayo whistled a random tune, twiddled her thumbs and looked into the air as she passed Alero. I nearly choked with laughter.

I heard Bolaji making high-and-mighty demands from Caro.

'I want to buy for all these girls. Don't collect money from them. I'll pay!' She was practically shouting as she took a bundle of naira notes from her bag.

Caro looked past her and smiled at me.

As Bolaji walked away with her entourage, Caro smiled and said, 'Same time next week?'

Bolaji put her hand to her chest as if it couldn't be her that Caro dared to speak to.

But she was right. Caro wasn't talking to her. She was talking to me!

CHAPTER TWENTY-TWO
GREAT MINDS

Princey had not been joking at assembly this morning when she said work would start in earnest. We did not even have time to celebrate Nile House coming second in the inspections, second only to Limpopo. By the time one teacher finished a lesson, the next was right outside waiting to start their own. During break, there was always some new thing for the Form One girls to be doing. Today for instance, we had our sticky buns and drinks sitting on the colourful benches that went all around the Great Hall, while Mrs Folawiyo told us about the famous women whose pictures graced the walls. Queen Amina and

Moremi the Great Warrior were my favourites.

'These women were brave warriors and fought for what they believed in,' Mrs Folawiyo said, stopping in front of Moremi, Queen of the Yoruba people with her jet-black cornrows pointing to the sky and embroidered with silver beads. 'Any questions?'

She looked at us fondly. When she smiled her white teeth shone brightly against her chocolate-coloured lipstick. She wore a crisp white blouse tucked into a brown A-line skirt that flowed to the ground, and looked every bit like a queen herself.

Bolaji shot her hand up. 'My grandfather is a great man too.'

'So your grandfather is a woman?!' Rashidat yelled.

I giggled so hard, I thought I would burst. Bolaji looked like she wanted to slap Rashidat.

Mrs Folawiyo smiled. 'I am sure you all have a lot of good examples in your families. Now girls, your next English essay is to write about how you could change something at the River School. Who can give me examples?'

Bukky's hands shot up first. 'I would change it so that senior girls don't ask junior girls to help them clean their classes.' Everyone agreed and started to chat about it.

'Yes, that's why they always win at classroom inspections.' Rashidat beamed as she collected high fives all round.

'I would like to see more girls at the River School who can't afford it.' I shot my hand into the air only after speaking.

Bolaji was right in. 'There are plenty of other free schools that they can go to. The River School is not for everybody.'

There was a hum of murmurs. Mrs Folawiyo did not seem fazed. She folded her arms and listened. 'The River School is for everybody! Not all of us are from rich homes.'

Flanky shot out of her seat on the bench.

Bukky and I got up to join her. 'Hear! Hear!' we cried.

'They are very tough exams that not many people can pass! So, I don't think it is open to everybody!' Rashidat was out of her seat too.

'Exactly!' Bolaji raised her hand to Rashidat,

who shook her head at her. They weren't saying the same thing.

'You all like to pretend you are not privileged like me but you are.' Bolaji did not sit back down.

'This is an amazing topic you have raised, Jumoke, I look forward to reading all about it in your essay.' Mrs Folawiyo flashed me her most approving smile.

I thought about what Caro had told me about Bolaji and a shiver went down my spine. I also thought about what Bolaji had said earlier. Was it true? Was I privileged and spoilt just like she was? I cringed at the thought.

I was still thinking about it at siesta, that quiet time after lunch when we all had to lie still on our beds pretending to be sleeping or reading a non-school book. I looked round the room. I tried to imagine Gemini on the bed above. She would be reading one of her American comics. On its front cover, several girls' names would be crossed out showing that they had read it. There were only three uncrossed names before mine on one of them, and I couldn't wait to get my hands on them.

Senior Funmi always slept facing the wall, so you couldn't see what she was doing. Tope lived for siesta, her nose glued deeply to yet another romantic novel. It too had several girls' names crossed out on the cover. Today's book was called *Garden of Love* and had a scantily dressed young woman in the arms of a rugged-looking man with a large scar slashed across his face. It was hard to imagine her interested in anything else but when the bell went for manual labour, Tope was up like a late-summer cricket, because she was in charge of giving the Form One girls their portions of grass to cut around Nile House.

'Come on, Jumoke! Grab your cutlass and hoe. You're going to be my assistant.' She emerged from under her covers, completely dressed in black sports trousers and long-sleeved top.

She saw the confusion on my face.

'Well, you don't want to be food for sandflies and mosquitoes, do you? See you at the back in five minutes.' By the time I got out, all the other Form One girls were gathered around Tope in front of the clothes line. They were all in shorts. It was a hot, sunny day but the Nile House cottage blocked the sunlight, providing a cool shade.

Tope taught us how to handle our implements. 'The cutlass is for trimming while the hoe can be used to get the roots of stubborn grass like this elephant grass here.' She pointed to a very large pale green weed that seemed to be rife around Nile House. She moved with such expertise as she plunged the hoe deep under the elephant grass and yanked it from the ground. We all cheered as she threw it into an old dry heap of grass.

'Be careful, it itches!' she warned.

Bukky, Flanky and I angled to get portions next to each other.

Clang! Clang! Clang! Our cutlasses crashed against the stones that were stuck in the ground. Suddenly, my cutlass made a duller sound and there was a scuttle beneath it. Tope jumped at me and pushed me away. She stood on a large stone and began to sway the bushes with her cutlass. The other girls started to gather.

'Move back, everybody. It's a scorpion.'

We all gasped.

The shiny black creature emerged on top of the

tip of Tope's cutlass, its tail curled forwards ready for attack.

She stepped down gently and flung the scorpion as far away as she could.

'Why didn't you kill it?' someone asked from the back of the crowd that had formed.

'Because this is its home, we are the ones intruding!' Tope was adamant. She continued, 'Now everyone, go in and change into trousers and long sleeves. Get a drink and come back in five minutes. Jumoke, you are all right as you are.'

She picked up a small white jerrycan that lay beside her. She put her face in the air and hovered it over her mouth. She drank a lot of water before handing it to me.

I drank just the way she had done.

'Thank you for the water . . . and for saving me from the scorpion.'

'No problem.'

'You weren't afraid at all?' I looked into her eyes to confirm.

'Nope!' She grinned at me. 'You thought I was a fear-fear, didn't you?'

I smiled. 'Well, yes!' I dared to say.

She laughed softly. 'My mother works on a farm. The River School is where I come to relax.'

'Tope.' I whispered her name.

'Yes?'

'You are on a scholarship, aren't you?' I asked quietly.

'Yes,' she declared with dignity. 'My dad invited Princey to watch me in a local play. You know who my dad is, right?'

I thought for a bit. 'No,' I answered.

'Baba Green is my dad.'

My eyes opened wide.

'Yes, the man that can make you crawl crawl like crocodile.' She threw her head back and laughed loudly.

I laughed too and then stopped to look deep into her eyes. Was it true? Could her daddy make us turn into crocodiles? Did he ride on top of a crocodile?

Tope smiled and added, 'All I can say is my dad would never wear crocodile shoes. Anyway, back to more important things. Princey was very impressed with my performance and invited me to sit for the River School exams. Matron was very against it. She made it abundantly clear during my fitness test. She said girls like me are not well suited—'

'Yes, that's what she thinks of Caro as well.' I jumped in.

'Oh, Caro! That girl can dance o!' Tope said.

'Yes, I wonder what would happen if Princey saw her dance too?' I looked at Tope hopefully.

'She is in Matron's care, isn't she?' Tope asked. 'I don't think Matron will have any intention of letting Caro go to school.'

My voice began to shake as I told her all about Caro and how she came to be in her position.

'I don't know why Matron has it in for good hard-working people when she has worked hard herself to get here.' I stopped myself from going further.

'I guess we poor people cannot help her in any way. Unlike Bolaji and her family.' Tope shrugged.

'Can you think of a way to help Caro?' I pleaded.

Tope bit her lip and thought for a while.

'Every Friday, after dinner, the Drama and Dance Society meet at the studio beside the home economics lab. If you can find a way to bring her, I will find a way to put her in front of Princey! We wear mufti so she should blend right in.'

I remembered how good it was seeing Caro at Shine-Shine River on Saturday.

'Can I take part too?' I ventured.

'I'm sure I can think of something for you to do.'

I was so overjoyed, I could have kissed her.

'Thank you, Tope,' I cried.

'Yes, Jumoke, you owe her your life,' Flanky declared, coming in at that moment with Bukky and several other girls and assuming I was thanking her for saving me from the scorpion. I smiled and nodded in agreement. Tope just might have saved the day indeed.

CHAPTER TWENTY-THREE

MIDNIGHT FEAST II

When I told Flanky and Bukky about my chat with Tope, we all agreed that we needed the help of our Form Two friends. Flanky was so desperate for the experience of a midnight feast that she decided it was the only way to tell them. We concocted an elaborate plan that involved a cryptic note left under each of their pillows. The note said:

> EXCLUSIVE MIDNIGHT FEAST TONIGHT
> Food sorted
> Nile Box room (GM, LF & the Twins)

We were so proud of ourselves as we walked to

class from assembly.

'I'm not sure I can concentrate in class today. Hopefully I won't faint from the excitement of it all.' Flanky ran towards one of the trees to touch wood.

I rolled my eyes and laughed deeply. I knew I was going to struggle as well. The only way I knew how to wait for something I was looking forward to was to rush everything. I rushed all my maths sums during the lesson and Mrs Aliu made me do them all over again, but I rushed those also and her shrieking voice must have been heard by all the fishermen on the river. I stuffed my puffpuff into my mouth at snack time but it was straight out of the frying pan and of course nobody spits out puffpuff so my whole mouth was burnt.

At dinner time, I tried to find out if Gemini had seen the note under her pillow but she seemed genuinely ignorant and just ate her rice and beans quietly. I had decided that this was my favourite meal at the River School so far. It was served with a fried tomato stew and little cutlets of beef that were as tender as could be. I cleared up everyone's plates at top speed instead of doing it with someone else and then skipped all the way back to the dorm. By the time it was bedtime, I fell asleep as soon as I hit the pillow, out of exhaustion.

Gemini tapped me gently and whispered, 'It's time.'

I managed to pull myself out of sleep. My bed creaked.

'Ssh!' she whispered. She had her pillow in her other hand.

I grabbed my pillow and a little bag filled with goodies I had bought from Caro's van.

We left the room on tiptoes. The moon peeked out over the lawn as if in cahoots with us. It was a very warm night and the toads and crickets were making a right old racket.

We were the last to arrive. It was only two minutes past midnight.

'Jumoke, where have you been?' Flanky asked in hushed tones.

'Sorry, I overslept,' I whispered back. I looked around the dark room. Bukky and Flanky had done an excellent job.

There were no candles this time. Just one torch shone in the middle of the blanket in the corner of the room. Even Baba Green would not have known there was anyone inside if he passed by. There were suitcases heaped up to hide us. The girls made room for us. We put our pillows on the blanket and sat down.

Nobody said a word as Flanky and I opened our bags of goodies. Between us, we put out two large sticky buns, a flask of tea and several plastic cups in the middle of the blanket. Lola shared out the buns so we all had a sizeable portion. Flanky shared out the tea, which was piping hot, and we stared at her in wonder.

'The senior in my room has a boiling ring!' We gasped. Those were completely against the rules.

'Yeah, don't ask,' Flanky added.

We ate in silence for a while.

I was the first to speak. 'So did you all know that it was when Princey saw Tope in a play in the village that she invited her to join River School on a scholarship?'

'Well, I knew she was on a scholarship and

Princey herself put her in charge of the annual theatre production. Last year's play was unbelievable. The props, costumes, everything!' Gemini was getting very excited.

'I thought of joining in this year but it is very demanding,' Lola added.

'Well, Tope thinks she can get Caro into the play somehow so that Princey can see how good she is at dancing. She's even allowed me to come along.' I was getting fired up and no longer speaking in whispered tones.

Tayo had been scribbling in her notepad and Michelle was hovering over her shoulder, whispering additions.

'Obviously, there are many things to consider.' Tayo raised her head finally. 'How will we get her away from Matron every Friday night? Won't people recognize her from the tuck-shop van? What if Matron is present at the performance, what do we do about that?' She peered over her spectacles at us.

My head fell. I'd known it was a long shot but I wanted to do something, anything.

Gemini got up and paced the room, which was

quite difficult as there were suitcases everywhere.

'I think we should deal with the first issue and address the rest later,' she said, scratching her head.

'Matron sometimes sleeps in the sickbay bedroom if there is a poorly girl she has to look after through the night.' Gemini continued pacing.

'Ah, I'm your gal for the job!' I was now used to seeing Bukky this way in the classroom. The others giggled quietly.

'What do you mean, Bukky?' I asked.

Bukky poured herself some tea. She drank it right down and began to hold her chest.

'That was hot,' she tried to yelp quietly.

She began to pinch both her cheeks repeatedly.

Tayo shone the torch on Bukky's face. She was so light-skinned, her left cheek had become bright red. She began to shiver and tears rolled down her face. I held her. She was red-hot like her face. I shrieked.

Bukky began to giggle. 'See? Fever on demand.'

We gasped.

'And that, ladies, is why I call her Pawpaw. Her face can turn red in five seconds!' Flanky whispered loudly.

Bukky giggled some more and we gave her a silent round of applause.

Tayo jumped up all of a sudden, peering down at her notepad. 'Let's do it!'

There were high fives all round. We only had a plan for this Friday so far but it was a start. Flanky and Bukky began to clear up.

Lola and Michelle stuffed all the leftovers into their mouths. We tiptoed back to our rooms, excited about our little scheme.

When we settled into our beds that night, I poked Gemini in the bed above.

'Thank you, Gemini!'

'You are welcome!' came a reply from the bed opposite. I turned right round. It was Ngozi. I smiled to myself. Gemini was already fast asleep!

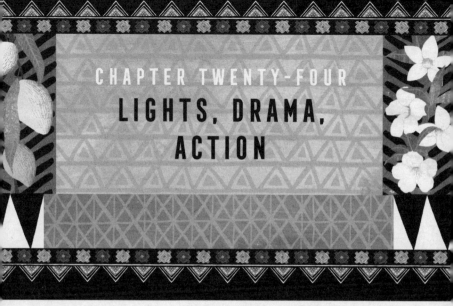

CHAPTER TWENTY-FOUR

LIGHTS, DRAMA, ACTION

Friday night couldn't come soon enough. Bukky, Flanky and I waited for our Form Two friends outside the dining hall. Flanky was armed with a flask of tea, which she handed to Bukky, who was a sight to behold in two jumpers and a scarf around her neck. She was already in character, refusing to smile and shivering. Today's dinner was a school favourite and scores of girls were flooding the dining hall for the yam pottage and fried mackerel. The smell of fish wafted through the air and my stomach grumbled. I spotted Gemini first and then saw Lola, Michelle and Tayo a short way behind her. I signalled to them excitedly.

'Oh no, Bukky! What's the matter? We can't do this without you!' Tayo said.

We kept quiet, watching Tayo, waiting for her to catch up.

'Oh! Well done!' She squealed in realization. 'You look dreadful!'

'Why, thank you.' Bukky took a bow and quickly returned to character.

Lola patted her school bag. 'I've got my note and clothes for Caro here,' she whispered, looking behind her.

The note read:

> Meet us outside the home economics lab right now. Matron will be away for hours. Don't be afraid!

Just then Michelle squealed in delight. We turned to see the reason for her excitement. It was Barky, her black-and-white coat shining under the fluorescent lights that surrounded the dining hall. She strolled casually into the dining hall, her tail upright and confident.

'She is always here for the *poisson*,' Michelle said. 'And I hate fish so I will give her mine.'

'I wish you'd just give me yours,' Gemini said, shouting after Michelle who was now trying to catch up with Barky.

It was Ngozi's turn to say the prayers. She stood tall in the middle of the dining hall, not in the front as other prefects had done. We kept completely quiet and shut our eyes.

'Plus God, minus Devil!' Ngozi bellowed.

I opened my eyes wide and looked around the table.

The 'amen' that followed was loud and full of merriment. Senior Funmi shook her ahead amidst the laughter, a small tear rolling down her cheek.

Once everyone had settled, we ate our food quietly. I looked towards Bukky's table, wondering if she had been able to keep it together in all the excitement. I couldn't see her. I nudged Gemini. 'I can't find Bukky.'

We both stretched our necks left and right, looking for her. We saw Senior Moradeke snapping her fingers while talking to Flanky and Lola. 'Run to the staff quarters and get Matron,' she ordered.

They ran out of the dining hall quickly. It was then I saw Bukky shivering even more dramatically than she had shown us. Her face was a bright red. She walked very slowly beside Senior Moradeke who put an arm over her.

I saw Lola walk back into the dining hall with Senior Moradeke. I could hardly wait to ask her how it all went.

When we were dismissed from dinner, I marched over to Lola and bombarded her with questions.

'Did you see Caro?' I asked eagerly. 'Did she look as if she was in trouble? Do you think she will come?' Lola sighed as we walked together to the home economics lab.

'One question at a time, Jummy. I saw Caro. She looked utterly shocked when I pushed the note into her hand at Matron's. I didn't have enough time to explain anything because Matron was right there, you know? But, I can tell you one thing. Caro is up to her neck in chores. There were clothes to iron everywhere.'

'Yes, she told me that she works from morning to night,' I corroborated.

I hoped with all my might that Caro would make it.

When we got to the front of the home economics lab, there was nobody there but we could see the lights on in some of the rooms and lots of movement.

'Look!' Lola whispered.

A few metres away, someone walked towards us, the light from the buildings bringing her into view.

'Caro!'

I was so happy I hugged her. 'I thought you may not come.'

'I nearly didn't, Matron has given me lots of ironing to do. I can't stay here for long.'

'Then let's get going.' Lola led us to the drama club room.

When we got closer we could hear all sorts of sounds: the piano, the flute, the tambourine and what sounded like the talking drum. Caro clasped her hands in delight. 'If ThankGod plays talking drum for you, it will be as if a person is talking!' she announced, almost forgetting herself for a moment. This was the Caro I knew from home. I was so happy.

We passed the room with all the music playing

and looked inside. I had seen many of the girls around school but didn't know their names. Reverend Folawiyo was in the front playing the piano along with them. We finally came to the drama room where Tope was holding a large stuffed crocodile to the ground. A group of girls surrounded her as she seemed to defeat the beast. Then she stood on it and everyone cheered. When she saw us, she flashed a wide grin. Lola and I waved. She came out to meet us.

'Great, just in time for the choreography.'

'Ehn?' Caro was confused.

'I will explain.' Tope blew the whistle around her neck and everyone in both rooms filtered out into the courtyard with their instruments. Many of the girls were wearing ankle bells that jingled with every step they made.

'Here!' Tope handed Lola a large box of shiny, colourful beads and some glue. She came back with the stuffed crocodile and dumped it in my arms.

'Stick all these beads all over the croc.'

'Why is there a crocodile in the play?' I asked.

'Because that's what everybody fears in this

school.' Tope said this as she handed Caro two ankle bells.

'Agbalumo seeds!' Caro yelped.

She showed them to me and, sure enough, they were dried agbalumo seeds bunched together with raffia string.

'We made them ourselves.' Tope beamed with pride.

She bent down to put on her own ankle bells and Caro followed suit.

About twenty girls formed a grid in the court-yard. The girls playing the instruments stood with us in the corridor poised to play. Tope put her hand in Caro's and took her to the front of the grid of girls.

'Try to follow everything I do.'

She blew her whistle again.

This time a soft piano tune filtered out from the room inside. I watched the reverend play. The boring man who taught us Christian religious studies was gone and in his place was a genius with his fingers. It was magical.

The flute began as well as the talking drum and the girls started to stomp their feet on the ground to different beats. When the tambourine joined in, the piano-playing became more intense and faster, and Tope began the most captivating dance I had ever seen. At first, Caro just stared at her with her mouth wide open. Then Tope nudged her to join in. Caro missed quite a lot of the steps but you could tell that with practice she would learn it in no time. Every time she got the hang of a sequence of steps, she looked at me and smiled. I smiled back, a warm feeling in my tummy.

By the time they had rehearsed several times and it was time to go, Lola and I were almost halfway through our task of beading the crocodile. I couldn't help noticing that the beads were all the colours of the houses at the river school. I also noticed that the orange beads far outnumbered the other colours. I was very pleased with that. Very pleased indeed.

Everything went to plan for the first two weeks. Each Friday, when Bukky developed a fever during dinner, Flanky and Matron had to stay with her while she slept a long sleep that lasted about three hours. Then, Lola and I would meet Caro waiting at the home economics lab. Nobody questioned Caro being there. They just got on with the rehearsals.

By the third Friday, Matron was having none of it and suggested that Bukky was allergic to fish.

'This girl, I forbid you to eat fish again!' She yelled so loudly Barky ran out of the dining hall.

Bukky had to double over to show she was in

real pain before Matron took her from the dining hall to the sickbay. We didn't know what we were going to do the following Friday.

Then one day after siesta, I woke up to find a large bulky thing hanging on the wall just next to the room door. It was covered with someone's orange bedspread.

I got out of bed to take a look.

'Ahem! Not so fast!' Tope looked up from her latest romance novel, *A Princess in Distress*.

'What is that?' I asked.

'Our star costume for the play. The better question would be "Whose is it?"'

My eyes opened wide. 'Yours?'

'Guess again.' Her eyes opened wider than mine.

'You don't mean . . .?'

'Yes! It's Caro's!'

I squealed with delight. Then I bit my lip.

'But we don't know how to get her to rehearsals any more.'

'You leave that to me!' She grinned cheekily.

The next day at assembly, Princey gave the microphone to Matron.

'Good morning, girls,' her cold, crisp voice boomed. She was in full matron uniform: white hat, dress and shoes with a shiny silver belt. You could hear a pin drop.

'I understand that there have been quite a few sightings of scorpions and snakes around the school. We have decided that it would be best for many of you to be trained in first aid to deal with the immediate response to scorpion stings and snakebites. So I will be training anyone who is interested every Friday evening after dinner in the dining hall until half-term.'

Bukky looked behind me and squeezed my hand. I squeezed hers tighter. Tope had done it again. Caro would be able to sneak out while Matron was busy.

Everything worked smoothly until one Saturday when the clouds were spitting out the last rains before the dry harmattan season.

Nile House girls were huddled together on the covered front porch of our house, waiting for the rain to subside so we could go out to the river. We could see Limpopo girls doing the same right opposite us.

The rain was finally dying down when someone let out a loud holler from Limpopo House.
The girl banged her palm against her mouth inter-
mittently to make a war cry. Some other Limpopo
girls jumped up and landed with a theatrical
thud. They had chosen their spot perfectly, right
on the passage that separated Limpopo from Nile
House.

Senior Moradeke stepped forward, her arms
akimbo, tapping her foot on the concrete floor.
There was a loud buzz of noise as we all wondered
what the Limpopo girls were up to.

Alero too came forward and mimicked Senior
Moradeke's stance. Bolaji followed and started to
chant.

'L is for Limpopo!'

The other Limpopo girls responded, 'Aye! It
doesn't get better than that!'

'I is for invincible,' Bolaji continued.

'Aye! We'll make you scram like a rat!'

'M is for magnificent!'

I had to hand it to Bolaji, she was magnificent.

'Aye! This is where the talent went!' They all
beat their chests with their hands.

'PO! PO! PO! PO!' they all shouted. 'That is the sound of LIMPOPO!'

They applauded themselves. Ngozi stepped forward so that she stood side by side with Senior Moradeke. Other Nile House seniors stood with them. Only Senior Moradeke spoke.

'Nile House girls, give them a round of applause.'

We were reluctant and our feeble applause was rejected.

'I mean it, Nile House girls.'

We made another attempt.

'Much better,' Senior Moradeke declared. She was just about to say more when there was a scuttle from the back, and some Nile House girls gave way for an orange-necked agama lizard that had pushed its way through the perforated bricks and landed with a splat on the cold frontage floor. We giggled. It thrust itself forwards in fear and leapt towards the Limpopo girls. Bolaji and Alero shrieked ridiculously which made all of them take to their heels. Lola's wild howl of a laugh echoed after them and the rest of us were in stitches.

Senior Moradeke sucked her teeth and walked

right back into the dorm. We all followed her until she turned back to address us in front of her room.

I could see why she was our house captain. Her orange-checked skirt and blouse were tucked in and pressed to perfection as usual. She was yet to plait her hair for the week and it was packed into a neat bun which gave her even more authority somehow. She looked every one of us in the eye.

'Nile House! Make no mistake! This is the term we win!'

I believed her. We all believed her. Someone raised a song I had heard before and we all joined in.

Winner Ooooooo Winner!
Winner Ooooo Winner!
Nile House you have won o!
Winner Pata! Pata!
You have won for ever! Winner!

The rain had now cleared, so we ran off to our river playground full of hope. An earthy smell of rain mixing with the red soil filled the air.

Tayo and Michelle took over the tuck-shop van

from Caro as usual and we enjoyed another Saturday together. We ran along the river fence, splashing water on each other. We taught some of the others how to play ride over, ride over. It was so much fun that we forgot that it was a non-inspection day.

I looked in horror as Alero dragged Tayo and Michelle towards us. My heart plunged even further when I saw Matron with Bolaji, pointing an accusing finger at us. There was a crowd of Limpopo girls in tow.

Caro was mortified and started to run towards the tuck shop.

'Not so fast!' Bolaji grabbed Caro's hand tightly.

Alero stopped in front of Senior Moradeke.

'Ma! All of Nile House are in this together!' She pointed at all of us as we huddled together to face the onslaught that would follow.

Matron addressed Senior Moradeke. 'What on earth is going on here? Your girls have turned into tuck-shop sellers while this girl, who should be selling, is prancing around with River School girls?'

The way Bolaji looked Caro up and down as if

she was dirt made me want to smack her tiny pointy face.

Senior Moradeke curtseyed. 'Please forgive us, Ma, I think the girls just wanted to help out.'

'Nonsense and ingredients! I will make sure that points are deducted from Nile House for this!'

Senior Moradeke's jaw dropped. Mine too. There was a huge outcry from the Nile House corner, most notably from Ngozi.

'As for you!' Matron turned to face Caro. 'You are here to do a job, you are not permitted to take time off. Just get in the van!' She turned and faced us all.

'That's it! Tuck shop is closed for the day!'

There was a louder cry from all corners this time. They directed their protest towards us.

Senior Moradeke walked quickly behind Matron, trying to persuade her to change her mind, but Matron didn't pay her any attention. She sucked her teeth several times and shook her head vigorously. Just before she got into the van, she glared at us severely. Then she drove off in a huff, red dust flying everywhere.

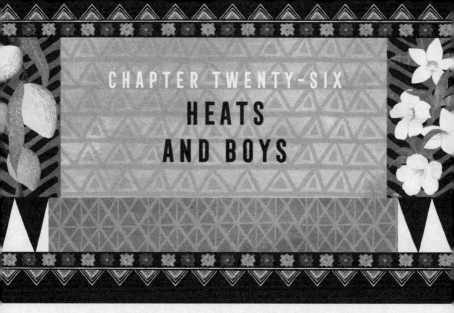

CHAPTER TWENTY-SIX
HEATS
AND BOYS

It was a very sober week for Nile House. We were the talk of the school for all the wrong reasons. We had caused the tuck shop to be closed and there were even rumours that Matron was not bringing it back until next term. To make matters worse, we had come fourth in the weekly inspections and in the overall points we were third behind Limpopo and Niger.

I was feeling rather down myself. I had no idea how much trouble Caro was in and there was no way to find out.

Both Ngozi and Senior Moradeke called us on to the lawn first thing on Tuesday morning.

Senior Moradeke's voice was husky and deep while Ngozi's was sharp and loud.

I could see from the heavy lump above me that Gemini had not moved.

'Hey, Gemini! Get up.' I tugged at her. She stirred and mumbled something about it being too early.

'Tope and Gemini, don't let me get to that lawn before you,' Senior Funmi practically barked, which was saying something.

I followed Senior Funmi out of the room, the sound of Gemini and Tope rushing about behind us.

On the lawn Ngozi was standing beside Senior Moradeke. There was such a physical contrast between the two seniors; although both were dark in complexion, one was tall and lean while the other was large and plump. They both were the epitome of strength and authority. Senior Funmi joined them so that all the senior girls were peering down at us from the corridors while we looked up from the lawn.

Senior Moradeke began to speak, her voice rough and deep. 'Nile House girls, first I want to say a big well done to all of you for all your hard work at the last inspection. We may have come third but we can still make sure we are the house with the most points at the end of half-term. We need to be the cleanest dorm for the next two weeks, the best at the Harmattan Games, and you need to be winning us points all across the school with quality work and good behaviour. A big well done to all the class-room workers who have earned us extra points. In fact, give yourselves a massive round of applause.'

'Up Nile House!' Ngozi roared.

Everyone yelled back, 'Hey ay ay! Nile House for show!'

Ngozi put her hand on her hip. 'Come on, you can do better than that!'

This time all of us shouted back. 'Hey ay ay! Nile House for show-oh oh oh!'

It was so electric, I got goosebumps.

Ngozi straightened herself. 'Speaking of winning more points, there are heats at the end of the week. So only Nile House athletes need to come out to run today. Jummy, you're coming along too.'

My mouth dropped.

'Yes! I hear you can be fast when you need to be!' She winked at Flanky. 'And Kingswill boys will be coming to train too, so I . . .'

Once she said this, everyone started chatting and giggling.

She shrugged at Senior Funmi. 'What's the point?' She left the lawn shaking her head and trying to hide a smile.

By the time we came back in from running, I was exhausted. I didn't know how Flanky and Ngozi did it. I may not get a stitch any more but it was too much work. Climbing the hill was the worst! I ought to box Flanky's ears for telling Ngozi I could run just because I ran fast when I wanted to see Caro in the van. Will they put Caro at all finish lines for the rest of my life?

I tried to dress quickly in my sportswear of orange shorts and white polo shirt with orange stripes. I joined the other Nile House runners on the porch. Ngozi had already gone ahead of us.

We met her on the sports field in front of the

assembly hall. She was talking to Mr Ajayi, the head of sports, and another man I hadn't seen before. Mr Ajayi was short and muscular with bulky calves that had several veins bulging through them. He wore a pair of brown khaki shorts with a white sports shirt. The other man had 'Kingswill' written on the back of his green sports jacket. That was when I noticed the field was littered with Kingswill boys. Many of them were talking to our girls.

'Just great! Kingswill boys!' Flanky huffed.

'One of my neighbours goes there,' I said.

'Just one? Lucky you. They are all my neighbours.'

'Oh yeah, I keep forgetting you live there.'

'Well, I'm not talking to any of them,' Flanky insisted.

Ngozi blew her whistle to get our attention. We all ran towards her.

'Good morning, sir,' we greeted Mr Ajayi in a childish unison.

He turned to face us. His face was small and his lips were an unusual colour of raw pink, almost as if someone had peeled the skin off.

'Well, what have we here?' His voice was rough, like he needed to cough.

'Sir, this is Flanky that I was telling you about.' Ngozi towered over both men, her long legs stretching from her orange skort for miles.

'If Ngozi says you are good, you must be!' He said this with a rich smile on his face. Every other thing about him was wild and rough but his smile was engaging. I smiled back and pointed to Flanky. 'She is very good, sir!'

The Kingswill coach spoke up. 'Don't I know you?' he said, looking at her.

'Yes, sir.' Flanky looked to the ground, embarrassed. 'I'm Francesca, Principal Davies's daughter.'

'Interesting, your brother is known more for his debating skills.' He blew his own whistle and several Kingswill boys came towards us.

Flanky shook her head and started digging her feet into the grass.

A tall boy with a mop of black hair covering his forehead led the pack. He looked like a reporter with a notebook in his hand and a pen behind his ear. He was not in sportswear like the rest of us.

He wore long khaki trousers and a dark green blazer.

'Flankydoodle!' he yelped fondly as he approached us.

'Flankydoodle?' I whispered.

'Gosh, Michael, why did you have to come?'

Flanky's brother ruffled her hair playfully. She tried to look annoyed.

The Kingswill coach grinned. 'This is Michael Davies, editor of the Kingswill paper. He's here to record our boys showing your girls a thing or two.'

Mr Ajayi quickly responded, 'And this is Ngozi Nwobi, Southern Nigeria's finest! There will be some teaching all right.'

The Kingswill coach blew his whistle again. 'Hundred metres fastest four.' He spoke to another boy, who started getting his squad together.

'I'll join in on the outside track,' Ngozi said.

'Me too!' Flanky added enthusiastically.

'You're going to race these big boys?' I was worried.

'It's win–win for all sides. They get better because they want to show off and I always run

209

alongside just to push myself.' Ngozi did not look as if she needed to push herself any further. I had no intention of doing any such thing but I wanted to see this first-hand.

As we were about to go to the start point, someone called my name. I knew who it was before I turned round. Flanky didn't wait with me.

'Owolabi!' I was surprisingly delighted. I don't know whether it was because it was a familiar face from home or because he was someone who knew how much Caro meant to me.

'I hoped I'd see you today.' He sounded so grown-up.

Some girls began to giggle.

I pulled him aside. He looked quite the sports man with his green duffel bag over his white top and khaki shorts.

'So what sport do you do?' I asked.

'Supporters club.' He grinned.

I laughed briefly before becoming serious again.

'You'll never guess who turned up here, at the River School.'

'Oh yeah, who?'

'Caro!'

'Oh wow, I didn't know she did the exams.' He sounded so cool about it.

'Aren't you extremely surprised?'

'She is very bright.' He looked around. 'So where is she?'

'That's the thing, she's here as a maid!'

'What!' Now he was surprised. 'Do her parents know?'

'It's complicated.' I sighed. 'But . . .'

Owolabi opened his eyes wide. 'Yes?'

'My friends and I have a plan.'

We walked all the way to the start point to watch the race and I told him all about Caro being at the River School.

'Well, if anyone can think of a way, it would be you!'

'Really?' It was the first nice thing he'd ever said to me.

'Yes, you always come up with solutions, especially if you want something enough,' Owolabi said, just as the whistle blew and the runners took their places. I looked around the field and my heart burnt within me. I couldn't shake the thought that Caro deserved a place here just like Owolabi and me.

CHAPTER TWENTY-SEVEN

SOMETHING TO RUN FOR

The Kingswill boys took the inside lanes while Ngozi and Flanky took the lanes on the outside.

'What about you, what sport do you do?' Owolabi asked.

I shrugged. 'I'm here for the hundred-metre juniors.'

'It's like I said, if you want it enough, Jummy, you always get it!'

He opened his duffel bag and pulled out an envelope. He pushed it into my hand. I scrunched it into my shorts pocket. I was still wondering what could be inside when the whistle went the second time. Michael came to stand beside us. 'Owolabi, you are not just here to watch. Get your notepad out!' He said this with so much authority that I nearly started looking for a notepad.

All six athletes propelled themselves forwards. The boys were really quick. It was as though the ground was shaking, the way their feet thudded on the track. I didn't take my eyes off the race for a second. There was something each one did that made them special runners. Ngozi did not look left or right and focused purely on the track from start to finish. Flanky used her arms and legs in the same way the fastest boy from Kingswill did and it seemed almost as if the rhythm from that added to their speed. The feet of the boy who looked like he would come second hardly seemed to touch the ground. It was exciting to watch. What was impressive was that neither Flanky nor Ngozi came last.

'We beat two of your boys!' I shouted to Owolabi and Michael as I ran to meet Flanky.

She was still out of breath when I caught up with her.

Ngozi sat on the ground drinking a bottle of water, grinning from ear to ear.

Mr Ajayi blew his whistle again and announced from a hand loudspeaker that it was time for the junior hundred-metre sprint.

'Jumoke and Flanky, you're both in this one,' Ngozi said, pouring water all over her head.

'I'm not sure about this.' I looked down at Ngozi and then at Flanky who was already stretching vigorously. She was relentless.

'Just imagine that Caro is at the finish line!' Ngozi winked. 'It's a sprint, not five kilometres. There's no time to get a stitch.'

Flanky nudged me. 'Or just look over there.'

She was pointing at Bolaji who was eyeing us from a few metres away. She was dressed in a purple skort and a white-and-purple polo top.

'I thought only seniors wore the skorts,' I said.

'Well, she looks too fancy to be a threat,' Flanky decided as we walked to join the juniors.

I could still feel Bolaji's eyes on me but I set my eyes on the track just like Ngozi.

Mr Ajayi blew his whistle and we shot off. Several boys were chanting Flanky's name with

Michael's voice the loudest. I kept my eyes on the finish line.

My body pushed forwards and I let the air into my chest. One foot had barely left the ground before I placed the other foot down. I used my arms and legs like I had seen Flanky do earlier and it thrust me even further forwards. Only one person was ahead of me and it was Bolaji. The crowd had gone wild. I thought of the beautiful times with Caro beside Shine-Shine River and how Bolaji had spoilt it for us. Owolabi and some boys were rooting for me and Ngozi was screaming my name with all her might. I shot forwards and Bolaji and I were now neck and neck. My arms were pumping hard and my breathing was fierce.

Suddenly, Bolaji pushed her chest out elaborately and propelled herself over the line. She didn't cheat, she won fair and square.

I crossed the line and flung myself to the ground, panting. I had come in second but my name was the one on everyone's lips. Ngozi and Flanky came up to me and hugged me. The girls from other houses came to cheer their own. Alero

and other Limpopo girls had hoisted Bolaji up
into the air shouting:

L.I.M. for the Lim, for the Limpopo
P.O.P.O. for the LIMPOPO
We have Bolaji who will win for LIMPOPO!
LIMPOPO!

Mr Ajayi blew his whistle so he could push
through everyone.

'These Form One girls are fast!' he said,
nodding his head enthusiastically. Everyone
cheered. 'And you, what's your name?'

I couldn't believe he was talking to me. I could
barely speak. 'Jumoke, sir, Jumoke Afolabi, sir.' I
held my chest.

'You are new to sprinting, aren't you?'

I nodded.

'That is the only reason you didn't win,' he
declared confidently.

I felt a wave of emotion as everyone cheered
again.

Mr Ajayi used his loudspeaker once more to
announce the heat scores and the effect on overall
house points. Limpopo was still in the lead but we

had now passed Niger House and were second. We cheered fervently. Limpopo girls shot across the field like they had won the World Cup.

As the crowd died down and girls dispersed towards other field events, I remembered the envelope from Owolabi. I unravelled it.

Owolabi had put the letters 'S.W.A.L.K.' on it. I looked quickly behind me. I knew what that meant. Sealed with a loving kiss. I sucked my teeth loudly. Stupid boy, he had done that deliberately to annoy me and he had succeeded. His main reason for writing was to invite me to Kingswill for their literary and debating day. Apparently, it was a thing. At the end of term, the school bus took you into Kingswill for a two-hour lunch on their school lawn after debates between us and them.

'Ugh!' I sighed to myself. I couldn't think of anything worse.

I decided to avoid him for the rest of the afternoon. But when the Kingswill coach came round, Mr Ajayi made all of us gather to say goodbye formally.

Flanky came and joined me.

'Flankydoodle!' I mocked.

She stuck her tongue out at me.

'I got in for juniors high jump, long jump and fifteen hundred metres.' She was so thrilled.

'Just the hundred metres for me,' I responded.

I nudged her when I noticed her brother talking to Ngozi, who was throwing her head back in fits of laughter.

Flanky rolled her eyes.

I laughed.

'Don't you start!' she pleaded.

The Kingswill bus roared into life and the boys got their things together and said their goodbyes. I was still wondering where Owolabi was when he stuck his head out of the window and shouted, 'Jummy! See you next week?'

I nodded as briefly as I could. There was a loud cheer from inside the bus. I was mortified.

Flanky grinned.

'I can't stand Kingswill boys!' I declared.

She put her arm around me.

'Jummydoodle! Welcome to the club!'

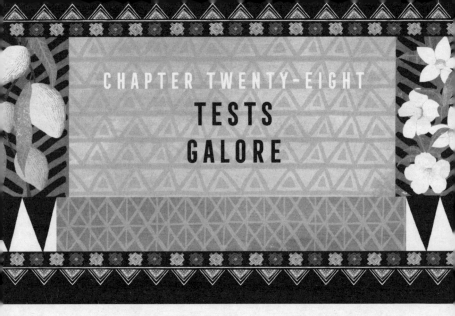

CHAPTER TWENTY-EIGHT

TESTS GALORE

The whole school had become very serious. We spent every evening in class studying and even when we got back to the dorm, we continued deep into the night preparing for tests. It was a big deal because if you failed any test, you had to resit them at the weekend while everyone was relaxing. Bukky studied well, underlining her entire notebook and making notes. Flanky asked her so many questions during study time that I could have aced the test just by listening to Bukky explain the answers.

It was a huge relief when Mrs Folawiyo arrived at form time to give us some fun news.

'I want to praise all your efforts in your school-work,' she said. 'Many teachers have told me you are a good class with a few clowns. Ahem!' She coughed. Many of us giggled. Some girls looked at Bukky and others looked at Rashidat who kept a very mischievous straight face. This made us giggle even harder.

'Well, you will be relieved to hear that school is very different, this Friday. It is cultural day where you will all dress in the different traditional attires from across the country and the dining hall will set out a buffet of exciting treats.'

Everyone started to speak at once. Bolaji raised her hand.

'My grandfather has sent different lace for me and all my friends to choose from. They are all very expensive but—'

A loud groan from all of us interrupted her. She tried hard to continue talking above it, but it was pointless.

Mrs Folawiyo interceded. 'Perhaps you could ask your cousin to pick the best one for you?'

Bolaji stuck out her tongue at the girls in the back and sat down.

'Are there any girls here going to Kingswill on Friday for the debate?' Mrs Folawiyo looked round the classroom. So did I. 'The maths teacher is giving out a free invite to anyone who gets full marks on her next test. I have one here for you, Flanky, and a plus-one from your father.'

Someone at the back made a snoring sound and we burst out laughing, including Flanky.

'So only Flanky, then?'

Flanky thumped me. I raised my hand quickly and put it back down.

Mrs Folawiyo smiled at me. 'I will be tying head ties outside the coach if you are wearing one.'

A few girls dared to put up their hands after that. I was pleased – there were about five of us.

Bolaji put up her hand again, her other hand rubbing her head vigorously.

'Excuse me, Ma, my head is really hurting badly all of a sudden. I have to go to the sickbay, I feel like throwing up.' She wrapped her arms around her tummy.

'That's very strange that you feel so ill so quickly. Go on to the sickbay then.' Mrs Folawiyo spoke to her really softly but I wasn't buying it. I smelt a big fat bushrat.

Our teacher continued to address us after Bolaji left, still clutching her tummy.

'You will be back in good time for the Drama and Dance performance in the Great Hall. I hear this year's performance will be outstanding!'

I thought of Caro and how rehearsals must be coming along. Tope no longer allowed me to watch and had sworn Caro to secrecy. I still saw Caro on Saturdays when she sold treats at the tuck shop. She was not allowed to leave the van now so me and the girls all bought stuff and exaggerated everything we needed just to stick around.

Gemini was the worst. 'What do you call that sticky candy again?' she would ask.

Caro would then go through each one, pointing. 'This one? This?'

Once, Caro said to Michelle, 'We have *les bonbons* today!' The way she said it was so spot on, I giggled so hard I nearly wet myself. I had seen a twinkle in Caro's eye. I was so happy that she was happy.

The loud cheer from my classmates brought me back to the present.

Mrs Folawiyo was reminding us that the Harmattan Games would take place next week just before the end of term. Someone started to drum. Rashidat began to sing.

> *Holiday is coming!*
> *Holiday is coming!*
> *No more morning bell,*
> *No more teacher's lip.*
> *Goodbye teachers, goodbye scholars.*
> *I am going on my jolly holiday,*
> *My jolly holiday.*

Smiling, Mrs Folawiyo picked up her books and left, making way for our next teacher.

We were still singing when Mrs Aliu's shrill voice pierced the air.

'Time for mathematics not music!' she said, slamming her books on Bukky's desk.

We were immediately brought back to our senses. And we needed them too because she set us a very difficult test.

'Jummy, are you awake, its only 5 a.m. and I can't wait to dress up for cultural day.' Gemini's arm dangled over my bed as she whispered to me from her top bunk.

'Yes, I wish we didn't have to run this morning, though.' I yawned.

'There is no running this morning!' Ngozi declared, throwing down her tent. 'This needs to be protected.' She pointed to her hair which was tied up in a big red scarf.

Tope sat up in her bed. 'No running?'

'You are suddenly cured of the illness you had already prepared!' Ngozi said.

This made Senior Funmi laugh really hard. It seemed nobody could sleep.

Tope pulled her metal bucket from under her bed. It screeched and everyone covered their ears.

Ngozi was already wrapped in a towel. Gemini jumped down and there was a general rushing about.

Some of Senior Funmi's friends came in with different traditional fabric and clothes.

'Funmi, show us your trado,' they demanded.

'This?' Someone dared to touch Caro's outfit on the wall and everyone in our room screamed.

'Sorry o! Gosh!' Senior Funmi's friend shook her head at us.

Lola, Tayo and Michelle barged into our room without knocking to show off their clothes.

'Just where do you think you are?' Ngozi stood with one hand on her hip, tapping her foot. 'Go back outside and knock!'

They went back out giggling.

This time they made a rhythmic knock and I could hear them giggling behind the door. They fell into the room, even more disorderly than before. Ngozi laughed and left the room with her bucket of water.

They showed off all their clothes. Michelle's was a red-and-blue dress made from adire fabric. She held out a red beret and modelled it for us. 'Very chic, very French!' she said, and we clapped.

Lola put her dress in front of her body and showed off the black sequins that outlined the neckline. It was very beautiful.

'Jummy, bring out your dress and stop pretending you are not interested!' Lola demanded.

I giggled and brought it out from under my pillow.

They all gasped in horror at my carelessness.

'Don't crush it!' Tayo said, freaking out at the creases already in my dress.

She opened it out and smoothed it over.

'So cool!' Gemini said.

I was so proud of my dress. Auntie Heather had sewn it for me. It was a beautiful emerald-green-and-black dress made from ankara fabric. It had a V-neck with a snug waist that then flowed out in an A-line to my knee.

'I have green pumps, neck beads and earrings to match,' I said.

Gemini refused to show us her outfit until after her shower. She shut her hefty padlock on her locker and folded her arms defiantly.

'I can use a hoe to jack your locker!' Lola warned.

'You better go and get ready!' Gemini marched them out of our room amidst giggles and fake protests.

When I was all dressed, I met Flanky and Bukky outside on the front porch. Bukky's dress was similar to mine but with a round neck. I smiled happily at her. Flanky wore ankara pedal pushers with a white cotton top.

'See? Nigerian at the bottom and English on top,' she said proudly.

It was a beautiful sunny morning and you could hear the birds chirping wildly in the trees. We walked to the dining hall in between many groups of girls all dressed up in delightful shades of green, purple, silver, gold and yellow. The buzz on the way was electric. Many girls stopped outside the dining hall to show off their dresses.

'Look!' said Flanky, pointing at Matron's van.

We walked around it looking to see if Matron was anywhere near it. Nobody was inside it.

Inside the dining hall, there was no food on individual tables. Instead, there was a delicious spread of sumptuous treats on the top tables. We picked up speed.

We filled our plates with piping-hot corn pudding served with moin moin cooked in green leaves. These were neatly arranged into a pyramid with one opened up and cut into tiny cubes with a fork beside it. One of the kitchen ladies invited us to try it.

'It is made from beans,' she explained to us.

'I'll have one,' Flanky said and we all grabbed one each and placed it on the plates provided.

'Thank you!' we chorused. She smiled at us warmly.

The next table made us leap with excitement. It had all the yummy treats that we usually got from Matron's van. Sticky buns, hot sizzling puffpuff and soft honey rolls. We filled our plates and went to the tea table. Mama Tea was serving hot chocolate and everyone was in the queue for it.

I was one of the last to get to the table.

Ngozi looked dazzling in a beautiful flowing dress. One half of the dress was black and the other half was a bright yellow. The two colours converged vertically to create a splash. She had tied her head with a matching scarf and her big black afro sprouted out in different directions.

'You look lovely, Jummy,' Gemini said, coming up behind me. Hers was a simply beautiful ensemble. She wore a black cotton trouser suit with red trimmings on all the cuffs.

'You look fantastic!' I reciprocated.

She twirled around to show it off.

'So see you on the coach at noon?' Ngozi suddenly said between spoons of corn pudding.

I nearly choked on my moin moin. 'Er, yes!' I said, quickly. Before anyone could ask who had invited me, Alero and Bolaji arrived in the dining hall with their entourage of girls in matching purple lace, just like at a wedding. Alero had a fan in her hand and they walked through the middle of the dining hall. The buzzing all around came to a standstill as we watched them strut past us.

'Everything is gone!' Alero yelped as she led her girls towards the buffet tables.

The whole hall erupted in laughter and Senior Moradeke used the opportunity to say prayers. She was her usual authoritative self, dressed loyally in orange lace.

'For the delicious food we have just had, we thank thee, o Lord!' We yelled the 'amen' louder than normal and everyone drained out of the dining hall towards the classrooms.

I was in a large group of girls when I saw Caro sitting in the bakery van.

I ran to her, making sure Matron was not about.

'Caro!' I called out. She turned and looked around her, a worried look on her face.

'Matron is in the kitchen, she will soon be out.'

On her lap was an open bag, full of purple housewear.

I looked at them and then back at her.

'Yes, Bolaji dumped them in my lap just now. I have to do laundry.'

I was so angry but I decided to use my time wisely.

'I am excited for you for tonight's play.' I looked in her eyes. She was so afraid.

'I am not sure about it, Jummy. Matron will be there.'

'Tope said she will take care of it. The last time she said that, it worked.'

Caro shrugged hopelessly.

'Just leave the house once Matron heads off for the show. Please, Caro.'

'I will try but—'

'You again?' We had not noticed Matron creep up behind us. 'Woe betide you if I ever see you with Caro again! What kind of nonsense is this?'

My heart started to beat very fast. The way she was yelling did not match what I had done. She turned to Caro.

'How many times have I told you that you are here to work, not fraternize with the school girls. You have a lot of washing and ironing to do today!' She straightened her uniform, turning to see how many people had seen her. Many girls had stopped to watch the commotion.

She muttered something to herself before hastily getting into her van and driving off. Caro did not look up at me again.

Flanky and Bukky were amongst the girls who

had stopped. We walked together to class. I told them what happened.

'It will be all right tonight, I'm sure.' Bukky tried to reassure me.

'Don't you see? Caro was already worried about leaving the house for the play. Now she will be terrified. It seems every time I try to help, I only make things worse.'

'I don't believe that at all.' Flanky was adamant.

'If you hadn't helped, nothing would have happened. At least something may now happen. Tonight will be brilliant!' She walked to the closest tree and touched it.

I wasn't convinced but I hoped with all my heart that Flanky was right.

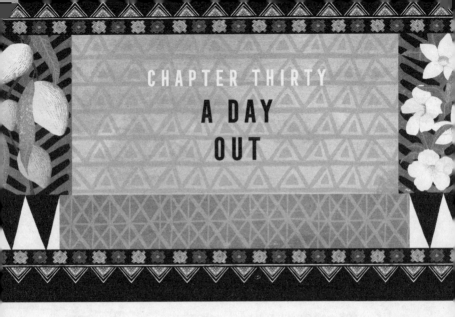

CHAPTER THIRTY

A DAY OUT

By the time we got to the coach for Kingswill College, a lot of senior girls were there. Senior Moradeke was there too. Mrs Folawiyo stood out in the crowd of girls in her red, green and yellow dress made from Ghanaian kente. She was helping the girls to tie elaborate head ties. It was gloriously sunny and the flowers in front of Princey's cottage matched all our vibrant colours.

Bukky, Flanky and I stood together in silence admiring all the beautiful dresses around us.

Bolaji appeared with her purple-lace ladies.

'Say hello to the girl with the highest score on

the maths test.' She twirled one of the plaits that dangled out of her purple head tie.

Bukky was straight in. 'How do you know? We haven't even got our papers back yet.'

'And you were not even in class, you had a tummy ache, remember?' I added.

'I did it under Matron's supervision and I'm sure I'll get the highest,' Bolaji answered smugly.

My stomach turned and I thought I was going to be sick, but Princey came out of her cottage and made me forget Bolaji.

I had never in all my life seen anyone dressed as gloriously as she was. She wore the full Yoruba traditional attire made from aso-oke. She was a credit to the top cloth indeed. She wore a cream lace top-and-bottom iro and buba underneath the gold-and-brown aso-oke. To my surprise and delight, she got on to the coach.

Just as we were about to leave, Rashidat came running on to the coach. She was waving a piece of paper frantically in her hand and breathing heavily as she tried to speak. 'I got the highest on the maths test and Mrs Aliu has given me a letter.' She handed it to Princey.

Bukky could not help herself. 'I knew it!' She stood up and shrieked. Everyone began to laugh. I looked over at Bolaji who was now looking very suspicious indeed.

Mrs Folawiyo stood up.

'Well, that's awkward, there is no extra seat. Mrs Aliu has left it too late. I'm sorry, Rashidat, but—

Bukky ran straight to the front and spoke to Mrs Folawiyo and Princey.

'Bolaji Oni, do you have a letter from Mrs Aliu too?'

Bolaji stood up. As she walked past me, she muttered, 'I am going to show your friend pepper!' I could tell from the look in her eye that Caro was going to be in trouble.

She stopped by Princey and said loud enough for all of us to hear, 'It's OK, Ma, my grandfather hosts several events like this. I'm happy for Rashidat to take my place.'

Princey and Mrs Folawiyo nodded in approval and Bolaji walked off the coach.

As the coach drove over the red bridge, I looked

down the river. I could see a large patch of red soil in the distance and it warmed my heart to remember all our Saturdays spent playing on it.

Bukky nudged me. 'Shine-Shine River truly always shines.'

I nodded.

The smell of bread from the bakery filled the air and Flanky whispered, 'I'm ready for lunch!'

'Grubido!' I whispered back and we giggled quietly. The coach turned left and down a very narrow road that made the coach brush all the trees on either side. I instinctively moved out of the way and Bukky laughed.

We arrived at Kingswill in less than fifteen minutes. Their school gate was just as grand as ours but once you got in, you could see the whole site. At least, that's what it looked like. The coach stopped in front of a large brown building and a tall white man stood in front of it with his hands behind his back.

'My dad!' Flanky whispered.

Several boys filed out of the large glass double doors behind the principal. Michael was one of them.

'Which one is yours?' Bukky asked.

'Ugh! None of them!' I protested.

Bukky laughed. 'You know what I mean.'

The boys were dressed in traditional attire as well but theirs was a uniform. They all wore dark green kaftans and trousers with the letters 'KWC' embroidered in a light green on the right. Suddenly, I spotted Owolabi. He was one of the last boys to troop out. He looked incredibly smart in his kaftan and what looked like freshly cut hair.

'That's my neighbour.' I pointed.

'Decent enough.'

We all got down and shook hands with the boys. Princey stood with their principal and Flanky introduced Bukky and me. We curtseyed and the Kingswill boys bowed their heads to Princey. It was such a dignified affair. Bukky nudged me. I turned to find Owolabi waiting a few steps away.

'Excuse me.' I curtseyed and left them.

I walked towards him, dragging Bukky along.

'Jummy! You don't look half bad.' He grinned.

'I am shocked at your neat appearance!' I quipped.

'Hey! Be nice!'

'This is my friend, Bukky.'

'I'm Owolabi and I know all Jummy's secrets.' He grinned as he led us through the double doors. Ngozi held one side open and Michael held the other. I smiled at Ngozi.

We were led into a big auditorium with chairs arranged on either side of the hall and a carpeted middle. Owolabi showed us to the seats allocated to the River School.

'See you after the debate.'

I nodded and smiled at him. Gone was the wild boy who sat inside the dustbin with ThankGod and here was a true gentleman. I put my green bag on my chair to keep a seat for Flanky.

After a few introductions, Mr Davies addressed us. 'I must apologize because you will have received a late change to the topic for debate today. It has become a hot potato here at Kingswill. "Shouldn't all education be free?" That is the question that one junior debater has been asking since visiting the River School. It seems he started a conversation there that made him question the injustice of some children being unable to afford the kind of solid education both our schools provide. I am very proud of this line of thought and we aim to address this injustice in the very near future.'

As he said this, he looked at Princey and she nodded to show her support. I looked at the other side of the hall and met Owolabi's eyes. He smiled gently. I think I knew who that junior debater might be.

'Without further ado, I'd like to invite our lead debaters to the stage.'

Michael walked in from the back, and there was a loud applause from the boys behind us and all down the other side of the hall. Flanky took her seat beside us.

Senior Moradeke too stood up and we attempted equal applause, but we were outnumbered.

They drew from a hat. Kingswill were to oppose the motion and we were to support.

Michael spoke first. He made very eloquent points on why education could not be free because of quality of education and staff, but when Senior Moradeke started speaking, she got everyone's attention. Even the way she introduced herself was outstanding. She commanded the whole stage. Princey kept nodding all through her speech. She made really strong points and ended by saying that she would not have stood a chance if she hadn't been given a scholarship and added, 'I hope I have managed to convince you – and not confuse you – that education should always be free.'

The entire hall rose to their feet to applaud her.

Owolabi led us out again on to the large lawn surrounded by huge trees at the back of the hall. There was an orchestra of students playing cellos and various other stringed instruments. Delicious canapés were being passed around by junior boys.

'So how are your plans going?' Owolabi asked as we sat down on the steps that led to the lawn.

'You mean Caro? The play is tonight. She's scared out of her mind.'

'I've written to my dad. I said it is unacceptable that children who live in our compound can't afford school and we do nothing about it.' Owolabi rose to his feet. 'I feel bad, to be honest. I haven't stopped thinking about it since I saw you last. At least it bothered you. I just accepted that I would go to secondary school and ThankGod would not.'

'I hope our plan works tonight. Our principal seemed to agree with yours on the topic.' I was trying to brighten up the subject.

The sun was going down and making pinkish patterns with the sky.

'Your school is truly beautiful,' I whispered.

He grinned at me. The band started playing the national anthem. We all stood for it.

Principal Davies thanked us for coming and praised Senior Moradeke once more for her contribution to the debate. He praised all of us and Princey beamed with pride.

As our coach drove off, Owolabi made scribbling signs with his hands, reminding me that I had promised to write. I nodded at him and smiled.

Flanky was the first to break the silence on board.

'Just my neighbour, my foot!'

Bukky burst into laughter. As did I.

In fact, that's all we did on the short drive back to school.

CHAPTER THIRTY-ONE

A NIGHT TO REMEMBER

'Thank you, girls, for a beautiful day out at Kingswill,' said Princey as we got off the coach. 'You did us proud. You can make your way to the Great Hall for the play. I will be in my office until it begins.'

The moon had made its appearance and brought all its starry friends along to crowd the sky. The air was dry and much cooler than usual and I wished I had a cardigan. I huddled up between Bukky and Flanky.

'You can feel the harmattan trying to creep in,' Bukky said.

In the Great Hall, girls were dashing about

carrying benches, palm fronts, painted cardboard and various other props. Some of the girls had painted their faces and decorated their bodies with white chalk.

'Oh wow! This is a real live set!' Bukky squealed.

We stopped in front of the banner with big letters that read, MOREMI, HERO OF OUR LAND, *an adaptation.*

There was a painting of Moremi with her big silver-beaded cornrows. She held a royal staff in her hand and pointed it up to the sky.

'Caro!' I remembered the fear in her eyes from earlier this morning. I remembered Bolaji's chilling words: *I am going to show your friend pepper.* I needed to find out if she had arrived in one piece.

The hall chairs had been arranged in segments on the left and right, with a round rug in the middle with little ornaments and small clay pots. The large stage was covered with a black cloth so that you couldn't see anything but there was a lot of noise coming from behind. I walked towards the stage. I could hear the flip-flopping sounds of girls' feet as they spilt in from the dining hall. The teachers had started to arrive. Mrs Folawiyo and her husband walked in hand in hand. In place of his priestly collar, the reverend wore a Ghanaian kente bow tie to match his wife's clothes.

I moved closer to the stage and peeked behind it. There were girls there but I didn't know them.

'Excuse me, do you know where Tope is?'

'She went to the toilet to change.'

But no one was in the toilets. I went into one of the cubicles just as two people came inside deep in conversation.

'That girl has grown massive wings! She shouldn't get away with doing that to Bolaji. She deliberately didn't do the sums right.'

'You trust me, the work I have given her today will put her right back in her station.'

The horror that ran through my bones when I realized it was Matron and Alero made me begin to shiver. And they were talking about Caro!

'I told her if she doesn't finish the work by the time I come back this evening, she will be in hot soup!'

Both of them laughed heartily and ran the tap

to wash their hands.

The toilet door opened again.

'Good evening, Matron. Hello, Alero.'

'Good evening, Tope,' Matron replied some-what curtly.

'You have worked hard on this play but you are used to that, aren't you?' Alero said.

'It's a shame your father will be unable to watch. He will be too busy patrolling the school compound.' Matron's voice was now really mean.

My heart skipped a beat. The way they spoke to her broke my heart.

I came out of my cubicle as soon as they both left.

Tope looked at me in the mirror, a small tear rolling down her cheek.

She turned to face me. She was dressed in a deep-burgundy aso-oke wrapper from her chest down to her knees, with a matching head tie. She was decorated with a burnt-orange bead necklace and waistband. Her body was painted with white chalk. She took a deep breath – I could see she did not want to talk about what had just happened.

'Caro isn't here,' I said.

'We haven't done her hair! I thought we could pull this off but I don't know what to do now.' Tope held her hands out to me helplessly. 'I have done my hair just like Caro's is meant to be, so that I can take her place if it comes to that!' She removed her head tie gently.

Her hair was just like Moremi's. She looked every inch the warrior queen.

My mouth fell to the floor. 'Caro is Moremi?!'

'Yes!' Tope cried.

I ran towards the main door of the toilet but ran back again. I felt like Caro's chicken. I put my hands clumsily on Tope's shoulders.

'Don't mind Matron and Alero, they are bullies!' I said.

I ran back out towards the auditorium. I found Flanky and Bukky right at the front.

'We kept a seat for you,' Bukky said.

'No time for that! Flanky, come with me!'

Flanky stood up immediately and followed me outside.

'What's going on?' she said as we got to the gravel path.

'Matron has punished Caro! I don't think she will be able to leave her house tonight. You know the way, right?'

Flanky didn't hesitate. 'Yes!' she said. 'Follow me.'

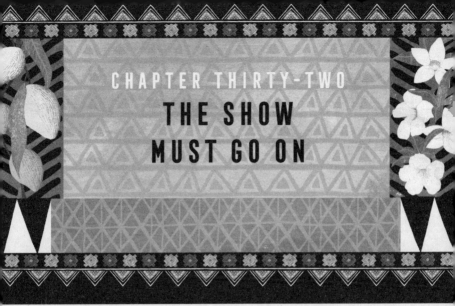

CHAPTER THIRTY-TWO

THE SHOW MUST GO ON

We ran along the tarred road that led to the staff quarters, as we had done so many times before on the morning run. Only this time Flanky ran faster. She took longer strides as if she was preparing for a long jump. I had to copy her to catch up with her. My mind was filled with conflicting thoughts. Should I report this to someone instead? What if all the adults felt that it was OK for Caro to be a maid instead of being in school? I kept hearing Matron's voice in my head: *Woe betide you if this happens again!*

Flanky was now way ahead of me. I sped up, taking even longer strides than before. I caught up with her as she took a left on to a tarred road with white cottages to the left and to the right.

'I can't really remember which one is Matron's cottage. It's either this one or that one.' Flanky pointed to two cottages in the middle and on the right. I bent down, putting my hands on my knees.

'You realize you're not even out of breath,' Flanky whispered.

It was true. I couldn't remember the last time I had had a stitch. All the training with Ngozi was paying off. I shrugged and followed her towards the cottage closest to us. We walked quietly to the side and peered through the mosquito-netted window. It was a kitchen with nobody inside. We walked along the cottage all the way to the other side. Still nobody.

'Maybe everyone's at the play,' Flanky whispered.

Someone switched on a light and I ducked and moved backwards, right into two large chickens. They made the most outrageous noise, flapping everywhere as they ran away into the darkness. Lights came on in both the cottages. We hid in the shadows.

'Caro!' Flanky pointed at the further cottage. I saw her.

We ran towards the window where she was.

'Caro!' I shouted in a hushed tone and Flanky and I instinctively ducked.

Caro came to the window looking this way and that. We lifted our heads. Caro pulled up the sash, still looking around. She looked very afraid as she whispered my name.

The way she was standing in the window reminded me of her selling food to the workmen at home. That Caro was clever and witty but the girl that stood before me was so frightened, I could almost taste it.

'Caro, can you open the door for us? We need to get you to the play!' I said desperately.

'Matron has not left any key. I cannot open the door.'

'So she locked you in? What if there is a fire?' Flanky protested.

'If there was a fire, you'd have to climb out of the window!' I said.

Caro understood what I was getting at.

'Ah Jummy, I can't o. Every time I try, I get

into hot soup.'

'Caro, please, trust me.'

She looked around the kitchen. On the dining table was a huge pile of clothes, including purple housewear and several River School uniforms.

She gestured towards the clothes. 'I have to starch and iron all Matron's uniforms and Bolaji and Alero's clothes before she comes back. I have been washing, cooking and cleaning since she caught me with you. I am tired.' She slumped into one of the dining chairs and started crying.

'Caro, please! Come with us. Maybe Princey will take a liking to you just like she did with Tope.'

Flanky tried to encourage her too but she was just too afraid.

'I saw Owolabi today.'

She looked into my eyes.

'He too is trying to make sure ThankGod can go to school.'

A little hope seemed to seep into her eyes.

I was worried when she began to laugh. I looked up at Flanky and shrugged.

'I did all Bolaji's maths sums wrong.' Caro's shoulders were shaking with laughter.

'What?'

'For her last test,' Caro answered smugly.

Flanky and I got it at the same time. We were still in fits when we heard footsteps and a light tapping. Fear rushed through me.

'Baba Green!' I whispered.

A lanky figure appeared out of the darkness and into the light streaming from Matron's kitchen.

We all gasped.

'E duro si be, do not move!' he commanded as he walked towards us.

I couldn't even move if I tried. Flanky too stood still. Caro backed away from the window. So this was why he was called Baba Green. He looked very different from when I had seen him in Princey's garden. Everything he was wearing was green. His kaftan was green, as were his trousers. Even his boots were green and so was his bamboo stick that he was still tapping on the ground.

His voice was rough and very strict. His eyes were set deep into his face and I remembered what the girls had said about him. *Baba Green at night is not the same as Baba Green in the daytime!* My heart began to beat faster.

'Sir,' I began to say.

I thought I caught a moment of softness and then it was gone as quick as it had appeared. But it gave me hope.

'We are trying to make it for the play,' I said.

His eyes widened.

'Tope's play!' I dared to add.

The softness in his eyes returned. 'You are not trying to steal sometin?'

'No, sir!' we all said at the same time.

Baba Green grinned to reveal a set of very white teeth that shone brilliantly against his dark face.

'This girl is going to be in Tope's play and we came to get her. We are very late!' I said desperately.

He started tapping his stick on the ground again as if he were consulting it. After what seemed like several minutes, he spoke again.

'Oya oya, come with me.'

Flanky and I looked at Caro.

'If ThankGod is going to school, me too, I must go!' She pushed her head through the window and stretched her hands out to us. Flanky and I pulled her slowly out and shut the window behind us.

Baba Green led us to the shuttle bus that took staff from the school into town sometimes. He was already inside tapping on the steering wheel.

We got in. Baba Green drove like fire. We arrived outside the Great Hall in under two minutes.

'Thank you, sir,' we shouted as we ran towards the hall.

It was dead silent. Not a single person in sight. Then in the doorway Tope appeared, her shoulders low and discouraged until she saw us.

'Caro!'

She grabbed her and rushed towards the toilet. 'Get me Senior Moradeke, Ngozi and Senior Funmi – if you can find them!'

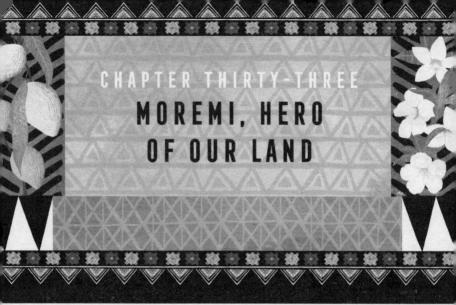

CHAPTER THIRTY-THREE
MOREMI, HERO OF OUR LAND

Flanky and I ran into the hall. It was packed. The ceiling fans were all on and the windows were open but you could still bake a cake in the heat. I spotted Senior Moradeke fanning herself with an exercise book.

As soon as I told her Tope needed her, she got up quickly. Flanky found Ngozi and Senior Funmi. All five of us walked quickly back to the toilet.

By the time we got there, Caro's face was already painted a glittering gold. She was dressed in a gold aso-oke wrapper from her chest to her toes. Tope was still tying it at the back with a beaded waistband. If I hadn't spent all my life playing with her, I would not have recognized her.

'OK guys, we need to be quick,' Tope said, 'I need to do six cornrows and cover them with these silver beads.'

All three seniors went to work immediately. Flanky and I just stood there in awe as they parted Caro's hair in different directions.

'Don't worry Jummy, we've got this now. Go and take your seat.'

As Flanky and I walked back into the hall, I felt relieved. I knew I had left Caro in safe hands. Our spaces in the hall had been taken but Bukky turned and saw us. She gestured to us to join her on the floor in front of Mrs Folawiyo and the reverend. There were several other Form One girls sitting on the floor in front of the stage. Matron sat right next to Princey. She shot me a look that chased all my safety away. What would happen to Caro after the play? What if our plan led nowhere?

Suddenly, the lights went out in the hall, leaving only the stage lights. The black cloth fell to the floor and two girls dressed in white bed sheets took it away.

The stage was magnificent. It was a market-place scene with stalls and sellers behind each stall. A spotlight appeared on the sellers as they called out to one another.

'Very good agbalumo you have there,' one said.

'Your yams are good enough for a royal festival,' said another.

There was a farmer using his hoe at the back. When the spotlight landed on him, we all laughed because it was a Form One girl dressed like an old man.

All of a sudden, from different parts of the stage, masqueraders covered in leaves came out and raided the market. They captured some of the sellers and carried their wares away in huge sacks, chanting as they went:

> *We shall conquer all the villages from west to east*
> *if you don't fear men, you will fear this beast.*

Then they hurled a giant crocodile on the ground. The huge beast with all its beads glowed in the dark and I smiled proudly.

There was weeping and wailing all across the

land. Someone sang a dirge while the spotlight landed on different groups trying to defeat the masqueraders but once the crocodile was raised in the air, all the people fled or fell down dead. The stage lights went out and the singing stopped.

The lights came back on to a grand palace setting with an elaborate throne in the middle. Guards surrounded it on either side. It was Caro who sat on the throne as Moremi. The whole auditorium gasped. She was stunning. She was decorated in gold paint from head to toe. Her hair was exactly like the painting of Moremi in the Great Hall. I clasped my hands together in excitement.

The sound of drums filled the air and Moremi stood up and began to dance, her staff in one hand. The dance mesmerized us all. She went low and brought herself up with ease. She curved her back in and out and twisted her waist so effortlessly. I looked and saw Princey nodding just like she had done when Senior Moradeke debated earlier today. She whispered to Matron to her right and to the teacher to her left. They all nodded in approval of this outstanding performance.

Suddenly, the dance was interrupted by the masqueraders. They tried to invade the palace like they had done the marketplace but they were no match for the palace guards. The masqueraders lifted up the crocodile but this time Moremi stood tall with her staff. The drums started to play. She snatched the crocodile away from the masqueraders, who fell down in fear. She wrestled the crocodile to the ground and stood on it. As each masquerader tried to get up, Moremi wielded her staff at each one and a puff of white smoke emerged from the staff, killing all of them.

The drumming became more festive as all the villagers entered the palace to celebrate and declare Moremi the Hero of Yorubaland! Then, the entire cast performed a flamboyant choreography led by Moremi and executed perfectly. When it ended and the lights went out, we all instinctively rose to our feet, whistling, clapping and cheering.

Someone raised a chant which quickly caught on.

All we are saying, dance one more dance!

All we are saying, dance one more dance!

The stage lights came back on. The audience roared in delight as the cast danced and sang a

Yoruba song to the beat of the drums. At last, they left the stage and we clapped so hard my palms were sore.

Bukky nudged me with her shoulder. 'She was unbelievable!'

'That she was! That she was,' I cried.

Tope came onstage to take a bow as the director, and we gave her a round of applause and refused to sit down. She announced each actor by their stage name. When they took their bow we cheered them enthusiastically and they remained on stage. Then we quietened down and she said the word that made us scream and shout and cheer the loudest.

'Moremi!'

The auditorium went wild. Princey and Matron were cheering too. I bet they were wondering who was behind all that gold paint. Matron would never think Caro could be so confident and talented. My heart swelled with pride.

'Moremi! Moremi! Moremi!' we chanted over and over.

Caro came on to the stage beaming from ear to ear and curtseyed.

Just then, I saw Bolaji sneak on to the stage and

stand with the actors, edging towards Caro. I saw her raise her hand behind Caro's back . . .

Caro started to fidget with her dress. Suddenly, she let out a loud cry, then a shriek. She yanked at the beaded waistband and threw off her wrapper just as a small pale green lizard leapt out of it. It stopped for a brief moment, nodded in its traditional fashion, then ran into the crowd.

The whole hall disintegrated into mayhem. There were girls screaming and running in different directions. That was when Flanky shoved me and nodded at Bolaji. She was giving her cousin a high five and they were laughing uncontrollably.

Something rose up in me. I thought of all Caro had done to get here. All we had done to make this possible. Without thinking, I ran up to the pair of them. I could hear Flanky shouting my name behind me.

'Bolaji, what have you done?' I yelled above the noise. 'You evil girl!' I was right in her face.

Alero raised her hand and slapped my face. I went wild. I grabbed Bolaji's headgear and pulled it off and in a second we were rolling on the floor in a real live fight.

'Stop this instant, girls!' Princey's voice boomed through the microphone.

Mrs Aliu tried hard to pull us up from the floor but neither of us wanted to be the first to let go. Eventually, I pulled away from Bolaji's grip and got up from the floor. I could hear Ngozi and Alero shouting at each other.

'I cannot believe Form One and my very own sports prefects are behaving like this!' Princey sounded more angry than I had ever heard her. 'Perhaps Nile and Limpopo Houses will be disqualified from the Harmattan Games altogether!'

There was a loud gasp, a murmur of protests, then silence as what Princey said sank in.

She continued, 'The following girls will most certainly be in my office first thing tomorrow morning to decide if they are the kind of girls who should be representing the River School! Alero Oni, Ngozi Nwobi, Bolaji Oni and Jumoke Afolabi.'

I was distraught, tears running down my face. I looked up meekly. My eyes met with Mrs Folawiyo's, and I saw disappointment all over her face.

I remembered Caro. I looked round, scanning the hall for her. I saw her with Matron and another teacher. They had covered her in a wrapper and she was sitting on a chair, her eyes red from tears and her gold face paint in a mess. Tope sat on the stairs of the stage, her head in her hands.

My heart was crushed. We had ruined all of Tope's hard work. What would happen to Caro now? Princey would forget about her performance and it made me shudder to think what Matron might do to her.

Matron whispered something to Princey. The head teacher's eyes were wide with surprise. She leant over to Mrs Folawiyo, who bowed her head. Princey started to speak, her voice still trembling with anger.

'It has come to my attention that one girl in particular is responsible for all this. Jumoke Afolabi!'

I looked up in horror. I sincerely thought she was going to call Bolaji's name. My mouth dropped. I saw Caro's look of shock too.

'I understand this is not the first time you have been disruptive in the little time you have been here. We cannot tolerate this kind of behaviour at the River School. Some girls may have to be excluded altogether! All of you are dismissed!'

With that, Princey dropped the microphone on the table and left the hall with all the teachers in tow.

I placed my face in my hands. I was in utter disgrace. This was the worst day of my life and there was nowhere to hide. I had let myself down. I had let everyone down. I hadn't managed to control myself. If only I had distinguished myself from Bolaji instead of behaving just like her. I wished I was like anyone but myself. And worse, I was all alone in this mess.

CHAPTER THIRTY-FOUR
DRY
SEASON

It was a cold, foggy day that suited the atmosphere at River School following the pandemonium of the night before. I could not make out any buildings or trees as I walked quietly beside Ngozi to Princey's office to face my punishment. I had not slept a wink. I kept having a nightmare vision of Caro and me trapped in a room filled with tiny lizards. We kept screaming but nobody could hear us.

Ngozi interrupted my thoughts. 'I can take any punishment as long as I can run for Nile House,' she said.

I wasn't sure she was talking to me. Her lean

body faced forwards so directly, it was as though she was talking to the clouds. I offered a response.

'Do you think they will tell our parents?'

'Hm! Yes, they probably will.'

My heart sank. Baba said violence was for those that had nothing else to offer.

'I tried to offer all I had and it did no good whatsoever,' I blurted out.

'Pardon?' Ngozi looked at me.

'Nothing,' I replied, shrugging my shoulders hopelessly.

'You mustn't be too hard on yourself. Those girls have been on our necks all term. I mean, if Princey hadn't stopped me, I may have been fighting on the floor just like you.'

I looked up at her and she chuckled before biting her lip wistfully.

We continued walking in silence until we reached Princey's office. Alero and Bolaji were already standing outside. Nobody said a word. The quadrangle outside the office was home to many beautiful flowers and plants. I was watching the lizards play amongst the flowers and thinking of the night before when Princey arrived.

'Well, if it isn't the ferocious four.' Princey announced her arrival, carrying a heavy handbag and several folders.

We jumped towards her and relieved her of her load. Ngozi carried the handbag and the rest of us divvied up the folders.

'Thank you, girls, do come in and have a seat.'

It was a very large office with several chairs against the wall. Ngozi and I drew two chairs close to the window nearer to Princey's large mahogany desk. Alero sat on the chair closest to the door we had come through.

'Jumoke Afolabi and Bolaji Oni, most girls don't see the inside of my office in Form One.' Princey's eyes were searching mine. I looked down. 'But I understand the situation better now.' I looked up at her kind face. She turned her gaze on Ngozi. 'So Ngozi Nwobi, can you tell me why I have called you here this morning?'

Ngozi looked Princey straight in the eye. 'Instead of defusing the situation yesterday night, I nearly came to blows with Alero here.'

'Well summarized. Alero?' Princey turned to face Bolaji's cousin.

'Yes, just like Ngozi, I added to the situation instead of defusing it.'

'But that is not all, is it Alero?' Princey looked at her intently.

The girl squashed up her face as if she had just bitten into a sour agbalumo. 'Ma? I don't understand what you mean.'

'I'll give you a few minutes to think about your response.'

Princey looked deep into Alero's eyes. She looked away shiftily.

'And you, Bolaji, fighting with Jumoke?'

Princey looked from Bolaji to me and then at Bolaji again. Bolaji didn't utter a word. She just held the principal's gaze with her usual confidence.

'Alero, have you had a think about why you are here today?'

'Yes, Ma. I don't understand why my own case is different to the others.'

Bolaji mumbled something and Alero shot her a look that could kill.

'What did you say, Bolaji?' Princey encouraged softly.

'Because of the lizard,' Bolaji blurted.

'I wasn't the one who put the lizard down her dress,' Alero snapped back. Ngozi looked at her in disgust.

'It wasn't my idea.' Bolaji defended herself.

Princey looked at Alero sternly. 'Out with it!'

Alero folded her arms. 'They started the lizard prank! They laughed us out of Nile House and sent a lizard after us. They bullied Bolaji in their room and—'

Ngozi straightened herself. 'That particular lizard appeared of its own volition.' She shook her head. 'I can't believe I am now speaking on behalf of a lizard.'

I nearly burst out laughing. I had to squeeze my lips together hard.

'That's enough,' snapped Princey. 'I have already decided what to do. I just wanted to give you all a chance to show remorse. You will tidy and weed the bushes and playground by the Sandy Hills and the Shine-Shine River. You will sweep the red soil and clear up all the litter. This must be done by the time the games start in a week's time. And Bolaji, you will return to Nile

House at the beginning of next term.'

Bolaji gasped. My heart sank. I had been nursing the idea that Caro may be given Bolaji's place but I knew it was only wishful thinking. She was probably in so much trouble with Matron that she might never see the inside of a school again, either as a maid or a pupil. What was going to happen to her? I had to blink several times to drive back the tears that were determined to flow.

'Yes, that was your original house. Your cousin did you no favours housing you at Limpopo. There may still be hope for you yet.' Princey looked at Bolaji intently but Bolaji didn't meet her gaze.

'As for you, Alero, that cruel prank ruined the night for everyone and it was played on a vulnerable young girl. Not to talk of slapping a junior. You will be relieved of your duties as Limpopo sports captain and I—'

Alero fell on the floor in a heap, wailing and protesting, her hands flapping up and down. I felt sorry for her but I didn't buy the dramatics. It was totally out of character. I wasn't alone.

'Get up this minute and face the consequences of your actions like a grown-up.' Princey's voice was very strict.

Alero looked up and met four pairs of eyes staring at her. Even Bolaji looked at her quizzically.

She stood up, her shoulders heaving up and down like an angry hyena.

Princey looked directly at me when she spoke again.

'A lot of what happened in last night's drama came from a good heart, but things always have to be done properly by involving the adults in your life.' She smiled at me, and I hardly dared to hope that I might not be excluded from the River School.

'That will be all, girls,' Princey said finally. 'I hope to see you here for better reasons in the future.'

No mention of writing to our parents or expulsion! I was so relieved I could have hugged Princey. I wished I had the guts to ask what would happen to Caro now but I didn't feel that I could.

Ngozi and I took the longer way past the staff

quarters to the dorms to avoid walking with Alero and Bolaji, who had been arguing violently when we parted ways.

CHAPTER THIRTY-FIVE

CLEANING UP
THE PLAYGROUND

Ngozi wanted us to start on the work immediately. We chose the left side of the
playground with the trees and swings and left the
right side for Bolaji and Alero. Numerous dry
leaves lay everywhere and several weeds needed
pulling out before the games. It didn't look like
we could finish on time.

I wondered where Ngozi got all her energy
from. Even though we were working daily, she
still found time to practise for the games. She
would tackle a section of the work and then run
round the entire playground raising red dust in
her wake. The playground was not the same

without Caro. I hadn't seen her anywhere except in my dreams. I hoped with all my heart that she was all right. Perhaps Matron had returned her to her parents.

Alero and Bolaji got a whole bunch of girls to help them and were soon way ahead of us, even though they started two days later than we did.

Senior Funmi sent Gemini and Tope out to help but Ngozi sent them back. I wouldn't have understood that before but now I knew Ngozi. She believed in doing things the right way and with all her might and with all her pride. I was so glad to know her.

On day four of our punishment, Bukky and Flanky came over after lunch to help me, armed with hoe and cutlass. Ngozi was in the middle of one of her runs.

'She's amazing, isn't she?' I was looking at Flanky who was admiring Ngozi.

'Yes, she is. When I'm in Form Four, I'm going to be sports captain,' she declared, beating her chest.

'I don't doubt that for a second,' Bukky said. 'But let's get started.'

'I have a better idea.' I put my cutlass on Bukky's cutlass to stop her.

'I'll cut the grass, seeing as it's my punishment not yours, and you can time me when I do runs round the playground.' I handed my watch over to Bukky.

'Time us! Time us!' Flanky was jumping up and down, pumped and ready to go.

So each day, after lunch, Bukky would arrive and time all three of us after Ngozi and I had cut a targeted amount of grass. Everyone started coming out to the river just to watch us. It was almost like a mini Harmattan Games. And every day, as the playground became tidier, we became stronger and faster. But could we win?

The day before the games, when the river had shied away from us because of the harmattan and the red soil had become dry clumps of sand, we stood on the hill admiring our work. It was the end of playtime and Baba Green's shuttle van was making its way up the hill. I remembered how he had helped us, and smiled. He was a very kind man indeed. I wanted to thank him again for helping us that night.

'What's that girl doing now?' I heard Ngozi ask with a hint of irritation.

I followed her eyes to see Bolaji walking on a fallen log with her arms stretched outwards as if she was walking a tightrope. She seemed to be lost in her own little world and it seemed to fit her somehow. She was on the side of the river without a fence and so close to the river shore.

Suddenly from the corner of my eye, I saw someone racing down the hill that was closest to Bolaji. The person was running towards Bolaji with all their might.

'Caro! No!' I screamed. I ran towards the river, my heart pounding out of my chest. I feared what she might do. By now everyone had realized something was afoot and I could hear their footsteps chasing after me. Some girls were shouting my name. Perhaps they feared what I would do too. I got to where Bolaji was only moments after Caro. Caro pushed me as far as she could and grabbed Bolaji's arm and shoved her in my direction. I looked up to see a large shifting shape moving slowly beneath the wet sand. I jumped up and pulled Bolaji with me. It was like she was frozen.

'Crocodile! Run!' Caro shouted at the crowd that was now moving closer.

The crocodile was no longer beneath the sand. Everybody could now see it. Its big grey body began to move in our direction. It was only a few metres from us. Caro and I ran as fast as we could, dragging Bolaji along with us.

Everyone screamed and made a run for it.

We all reached the top of the hills, still hollering and out of breath. The shuttle van raced back down the hill honking its horn and Baba Green parked in such a way that we couldn't see anything. Girls stretched their necks like giraffes to see what would happen to the crocodile but nobody could catch a glimpse.

'Bolaji! Bolaji!' Alero arrived, screeching at the top of her voice. 'Why are you allowing that girl to touch you?'

I didn't care if she was a senior girl. I was going to answer her back.

'Caro saved Bolaji from a crocodile!'

The crowd cheered.

Bolaji yanked her hand away from Caro's. Caro looked hurt.

The crowd booed.

'What were you expecting, some kind of trophy?' Bolaji quipped.

Everybody protested and began to talk at once. The shuttle van began to move again and everybody turned towards it. We all wanted to see what had become of the crocodile. Baba Green called over some prefects and spoke to them. The noise had started to die down but Caro had disappeared and so had Bolaji and Alero. I looked for them in the crowd but nobody had seen them leave. I was distraught. Ngozi put her hand on my shoulder.

'You are not like Bolaji at all.' She spoke very softly for a change.

I couldn't help myself. Everything just came tumbling out.

'Bolaji cheated on her entrance exams! Matron showed her the questions.'

'What?' Ngozi gasped. 'How do you know this?'

I told her everything. She nodded and shook her head in all the right places.

The next thing I knew she had gathered the crowd and led them in a chant. At first, I couldn't make it out and then I did.

> *What would it look like*
> *if all of us came together*
> *to help Caro succeed!*

It was the question Princey had asked at the first assembly of term. Tears filled my eyes as I joined Ngozi at the front. We carried on chanting and marched all the way to Princey's cottage.

Princey came out to see what the noise was about. She was accompanied by Reverend Folawiyo and Principal Davies. By this time, Flanky and Bukky were with me in the front. We continued our chant.

> *What would it look like*
> *if all of us came together*
> *to help Caro succeed!*

Ngozi walked boldly up to the three adults and spoke to them. They were all nodding their heads and speaking in hushed tones. We continued to chant.

Senior Moradeke and a few other seniors joined the adults. We could not tell if they were angry with us or not.

A few other teachers came out from the staff quarters.

'OK, settle down girls, and listen.' Princey's voice was firm but did not seem angry.

The crowd became silent.

'First, I have to ask you all to stay away from the playground and river area for the rest of the term. I have to also say that I am very proud of you all. Not only have you conducted a peaceful protest but you have done it for something beyond your own immediate needs.'

Principal Davies whispered something to her.

She smiled. 'Yes. We were just deciding now that our two schools need to work together to ensure a fairer entry process, so that children from every walk of life can get the chance of a great education.' Princey paused for a moment before continuing.

'Now you ask me what it would look like if all of us came together to help Caro succeed? Just look around you.'

I looked around me. Dusk was falling and I saw beams of torches scattered far and wide. I knew that most of the school was now here.

'This is what it would look like!' Princey held out her hands towards us.

We cheered louder than I had ever heard at the River School.

'Girls, leave this situation with the adults. We will do our best to come to a fair decision for all concerned,' Princey said as we quietened down. The dinner bell rang and we made our way to the dining hall.

Ngozi put her arm around me as we walked.

'I saw you running after Caro,' she said. 'Not bad at all, Afolabi, not bad at all!' A pensive smile formed on her lips. Whatever she was thinking, it felt so good to have her in my corner.

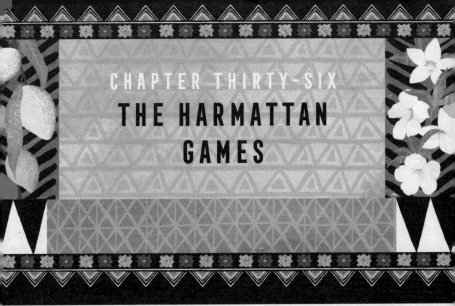

CHAPTER THIRTY-SIX

THE HARMATTAN GAMES

It was a perfect harmattan morning on the day of the games. The fog outside made everything disappear but we hoped with all our hearts that the sun would soon break out and conquer it.

Nile House was heaving with pride and enthusiasm. Ngozi looked like a winner already in her crisp white shorts and orange top. Her running shoes were a brilliant white and she packed her fierce hair in a wild bun.

I got dressed too and Flanky came to join us.

Gemini began shrieking. 'Go, Nile House! Go, Nile House, go!'

Everyone cheered.

I smiled to myself as I stared up at the Moremi costume hanging on the wall. It was only a few days until the holidays when I'd hopefully see Caro again. Princey had said we should trust her to do the right thing and I felt sure that at least Caro would be returned home.

Parents were already arriving and everyone was excited. Occasionally, someone would shout a girl's name on the front porch and announce her family had arrived. There would be a rushing of feet and shrieks of happiness as the girl made her way to see her parents. There was no announcement for me yet so I went to the stadium with Flanky and other Nile House athletes.

The sun now shone brilliantly and the new stadium looked spectacular. It was an oval shape with a red eight-lane track running around a vibrant green infield. Two long jump pits stretched out in front of the spectators' stand and a tall throwing cage covered in bright green netting stood at one end. Next to the discus cage, Senior Moradeke practised her shot-put from the throwing circle. She looked grand in her white skort and orange top. Ngozi was talking to Mr

Ajayi at the sandpit for the long jump and Flanky took off towards them. The rest of us sat around the competition stand, opposite the covered pavilion where the parents, staff, visiting schools and River School girls sat.

I kept looking to see if Baba and Mummy had arrived. It would be difficult to see them amongst the growing crowd. I was excited about seeing them after so long but I was equally worried about the race. Would I win for Nile House? And did I dare dream that Nile House would break Limpopo's winning streak?

I was glad when I finally spotted familiar faces. Baba and Mummy were here! Right next to them was a face that made my heart leap with even more excitement. It was Caro's dad! I ran towards the pavilion and climbed through the crowds, waving my hands at them. They didn't see me, so I went to the iron bars that separated the parents from the girls.

'Baba! Mummy!'

The three of them looked in my direction and smiled.

'My precious child!' Caro's dad shouted above

the noise. He was in a smart white shirt tucked into black trousers. I had hardly ever seen him in anything but a white singlet and rolled up trousers. He clasped my hands in his.

'Good afternoon, sir,' I said. 'What of Caro, sir?'

They pointed behind me. I turned to see Caro coming out of the tunnel that separated the Nile House and Limpopo seats. She was in a very smart white dress. Gone was the scruffy blue pinafore. My heart raced with glee. I looked back at them, my eyes full of questions.

Caro's dad was close to tears. He whispered loudly, 'Because of you, Caro will be staying at the River School.'

My face broke into a thousand smiles. 'But how, sir?' I asked. I wanted to know if she would be here as a pupil or as a maid.

Mummy intervened. 'Jumoke, there is so much to explain but we can do that after the games, can't we?' She winked at me, so I left it at that.

I hugged Baba even though the iron barrier stood between us.

'You have done us proud, Jumoke. And . . .' He reached over the iron bar to rub my head fondly.

'Since when were you an athlete?' He grinned.

I grinned back. My heart swelled with pride.

'Go and show me what you've got,' Baba said.

I ran back through the noisy crowd to my team, bumping into Bukky on the way.

'Hey, did you see Caro?' I shouted.

'Yes, you're the only one that didn't know she was going to be here today.' She winked mischievously.

'No way!' I cried.

'It was a surprise, Senior Funmi made us promise.'

She stuck out her tongue at me and I made a face at her and ran to join the other Nile House athletes.

The whole stadium joined hands as Princey announced the opening of the Harmattan Games with the singing of the school song.

We sang the last few lines with so much gusto, I thought I'd lose my voice.

Together, we truly shine
For victory is yours and mine.
Shine River School, River School shine!

Mr Ajayi blew his whistle and announced that the fifteen hundred metres would be the first race. Flanky stood up and stretched. I caught her eye and gave her a thumbs-up. She took her position and the whistle blew. They would be going round almost four times so everyone focused on the events in the middle of the track. Senior Moradeke yelled extremely loudly as she threw her shot-put. I saw Caro walking towards me. I ran to her.

'Caro, I saw your dad. You are staying at River School!' I was hardly coherent. 'I am so glad to see you. I was so worried for you!'

'Yes, last night Princey sent for Matron. That was the last time I saw her. After a few hours, Princey sent for me too. Matron has been asked to leave River School. She went this morning. I slept in the house captain's room in Congo House.'

'Princey kept her word.' I smiled.

'That's not all. Bolaji has been asked to leave too.'

My mouth hung open. I was shocked. I didn't see that coming. I actually thought she was above the law.

'Her father came for her last night after Princey called all our parents,' Caro continued. 'She told your dad to bring my dad. After meeting my dad, Princey has agreed to let me stay at River School on a full scholarship!'

I jumped into Caro's arms.

'Caro! That is amazing!' Tears formed in both our eyes.

'I haven't told you the best part, Jummy!' Caro announced excitedly.

'There's more?' I said, as wide-eyed as an owl.

She leant in and whispered in my ear. 'From today I am going to be in Nile House, room one!'

'No!' I screamed in disbelief.

'Yes!' Caro yelled.

We hugged each other, jumping up and down. I could no longer blink back the tears.

Suddenly, the roars of the crowd grew louder and I knew it must be the last lap of Flanky's race. I dragged Caro to a better spot.

When Flanky passed by our team, we yelled at the top of our voices.

'Flank-y! Flank-y!'

She was in second position just behind Senegal.

She looked back just in time to see the Limpopo girl almost go past her. It was just what she needed. She leapt forward fiercely.

As she came round the bend to the final straight, Flanky propelled herself forwards and accelerated past the Senegal girl, winning by more than a few seconds. We went wild. Ngozi had to stop us from running on to the track.

'Flanky! Flanky!' we all roared. Caro was shouting at the top of her voice too.

Next was my hundred-metre race and I came second to Limpopo.

And that was how it was all day. Limpopo would win one or two races and then Nile House would win a couple more, mostly thanks to Ngozi and Flanky. The rivalry was fierce and we sang many songs to that effect. We were still in the throes of chanting when Mr Ajayi picked up his loudspeaker again.

'Now for the race we have all been waiting for. The four by hundred metres mixed relay, both seniors and juniors combined.'

The roar from the crowd was the loudest it had been all day. Everyone went back to their seats and the whole stadium was quiet.

Mr Ajayi continued, 'This last race is particularly important because although Limpopo is in the lead in terms of overall points this term, Nile House can still win if they win this race and get a few more points from the shot-put and discus.'

A quiet murmur ran through the stadium.

I shot Flanky a look. Her face said it all. She reached over to touch a wooden beam. I grinned at her.

Alero went to the last leg for Limpopo. Ngozi came running to me instead of taking her position.

'Afolabi, I want you on the last leg instead of me.'

'Me?' I was worried.

'Yes you! You can do it. Some of our runners need a break so I'm switching things up. We will give you a great start and then you can finish it off.'

'But against a senior, though?' I continued to protest.

'Sometimes smaller is better.' Ngozi looked deep into my eyes. I knew there was no use arguing with her.

I walked slowly to the last leg position and stood beside Alero. She shot me the look of death.

Ngozi's words were still ringing in my ears. *Sometimes, smaller is better.*

Mr Ajayi's whistle pierced the pregnant silence in the stadium and Ngozi was off. She left everyone behind and passed the baton to Flanky. The crowd cheered ecstatically. She in turn passed it triumphantly to the third leg and she too ran fiercely but the Limpopo girl was extremely fast and overtook Nile House, passing the baton to Alero at least three paces before the baton got to me. The crowd had totally lost it. People were screaming as if it were the Olympics. I snatched the baton from my colleague and gave chase with all my might.

Sometimes, smaller is better!

I pushed my body to take longer strides and my feet bounced off the ground as if I were running on hot coals. There was no one in that stadium but me. I could hear nothing but my own heartbeat and Ngozi's words.

Sometimes, smaller is better!

I was nearly neck and neck with Alero. She

looked back at me and that was my chance. I seized the moment and let the finish line come to me. Just before I stepped over the line, I dipped my chest forward just as I had seen Ngozi do last week on the playground and Limpopo lost by an eyelash!

The crowd erupted.

Mr Ajayi came running towards the athletes in orange, shouting into his loudspeaker.

'Nile House wins!'

Yes! We had done it. All of us had done it!

Ngozi carried me into the air and I saw other Nile House girls run on to the track. Nobody could stop them. Caro was running towards me. I looked into the crowd. Baba and Caro's dad had gone wild with excitement. Everyone was chanting.

> *Winner o! Winner! Winner o! Winner!*
> *Nile House you have won o!*
> *Winner!*
> *Pata Pata! You have won for ever!*
> *Winner!*

Finally, Princey mounted the podium and we

were silent.

She spoke about how hard we had all worked this term. Then she announced the results so that she could hand out the trophies formally. All Nile House girls held hands, our hearts beating wildly.

'In third place, Niger House!'

The crowd applauded and the Niger sports captain with a large group of girls in green came forward to collect their trophy.

Princey continued when we had quietened down again.

'In second place, Limpopo.' We all applauded vigorously and Senior Moradeke clapped with her hands in the air as a sea of girls in purple came forward to take their trophy. Alero was nowhere in sight.

Princey looked round at all the athletes and smiled.

'I have waited to say this for a very long time! It is with immense pride that I formally announce that the overall winners of the River School Harmattan Games are Nile House!'

The whole of Nile House dispersed on to the tracks and Ngozi grabbed my hand in hers to collect the trophy with her and Senior Moradeke. I was barely visible between the two of them as we raised the silver cup in the air to more shouts from the crowd and Nile House. This was the best day of my life. I was proud of myself. Proud of what we had all done. I was proud of my passion for running and overjoyed to be part of this amazing house. Tears ran down my face. All my friends were around me and all the adults in my life were proud of me.

Princey began to lead us in the school song for the second time that day, and we roared the last lines like drunken soldiers who had just won the war.

Together, we truly shine
For victory is yours and mine
Shine River School, River School shine!

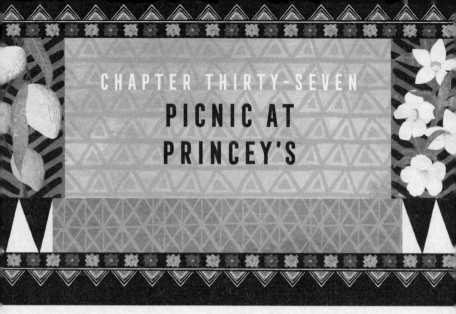

CHAPTER THIRTY-SEVEN

PICNIC AT PRINCEY'S

It was the day before the half-term holidays and we couldn't have asked for a better day to be sprawled across Princey's lawn for a delectable array of treats. The sun was blazing and the harmattan winds were in just the right mood to keep our orange-checked bedspreads intact on the freshly cut grass. The noise was electric with laughter and games. Lola chased Gemini round the back of the lawn and Tayo shouted after them, 'Girls, you promised to play quiz with me!'

Others were showing off their skills with the skipping rope, to the beat of different songs coming from Princey's front porch.

The Form One girls were responsible for bringing the treats out for their own rooms. Caro and I were carrying the sizzling bowl of hot puffpuff out when Mama Tea cried, 'Wait, I haven't put sugar.' She poured a lavish amount of granulated sugar on our bowl of puffpuff which made them glisten. She winked at us. 'Well done, girls.'

Gemini ran over when she saw us return with the bowl.

'I'll have some of that!' She bit into one, revealing its soft inner flesh.

Senior Funmi grabbed another. 'These are delicious. Go and bring more!'

The shuttle bus arrived with Mrs Folawiyo and Mrs Aliu.

'We need some girls to carry the cake,' they announced.

There was a loud cheer. Flanky and Bukky hurried towards them. Tope ran up to the shuttle bus too but went to the driver's side.

Caro and I went back in and brought freshly fried chicken and jollof rice individually packed, cupcakes, biscuits, oranges, mango slices and freshly made lemonade with ice. We set them all on my orange bedspread that was laid on the lawn.

The ice was a hit with Ngozi who crunched one of the cubes in her mouth before pouring the rest over her head. She squealed with glee as the ice cooled her down from the heat. Now that Nile House had won, Ngozi was always in a good mood.

'Only you, Ngozi Nwobi!' Senior Funmi chuckled.

Ngozi threw her head back in a fit of laughter.

Tope helped her dad carry a table from the shuttle van.

I got up from the lawn to greet him.

'Thank you, sir, for driving us to the play that night,' I said.

'Yes, sir, thank you very much,' Caro said, curtseying at the same time.

'It was good to be of help to Tope's friends,' Baba Green said.

Gemini whispered to Lola rather loudly, 'Crawl crawl like crocodile.'

'Sharap, Gemini!' Senior Ngozi said in between giggles.

Baba Green shook his head fondly and walked back towards the shuttle van with Tope.

Princey and Mrs Aliu emerged from the cottage in deep conversation. Senior Moradeke was right behind them carrying an enormous tower of agbalumos. There was a loud shout of joy at the sight of them.

Caro's tummy rumbled.

'Grubido!' everyone in the vicinity shouted at the same time.

Mrs Aliu started to speak, her shrill voice piercing deep down within us.

'I am so proud of you Nile House girls. I have certificates to give to one girl per room who the prefects feel did a little bit extra this term.'

She gave the envelopes to Princey who read them out.

'Nile House, room one – Tope Lawanson. For the production of *Moremi*.'

Everyone cheered really hard for Tope. I cheered the loudest. She was the one who had dared to believe Caro could join the River School just as she had, plus I couldn't forget the scary scorpion she saved me from. Tope got up, turned to everyone and took an exaggerated bow. We hooted with laughter.

Gemini shouted, 'Madam Drama!'

We all cheered for the room awards as if it were us receiving them.

'Nile House room nine – Bukky Adeyemi, highest classroom points.'

Bukky was extremely pleased with this and shouted, 'Up Form One O!' She wriggled her waist and danced all the way to the front. She got a nod of approval from Mrs Folawiyo when she accepted her certificate.

When all the awards had been given, Senior Moradeke whispered to Princey who flashed her deepest smile and gave way for her to speak.

'I have a special gift for someone who has had a few hard knocks this term, but has managed to look beyond herself for the greater good of the team and for her friends.' Senior Moradeke paused and then smiled as she said, 'Jumoke Afolabi.'

The whole lawn cheered. I was not expecting that. I was very close to tears.

Flanky shouted, 'Efiko sprinter!'

'Efiko friend!' Ngozi added.

There was a loud roar of agreement.

I walked up meekly to collect my gift but Senior Moradeke's hands were empty. 'Take as many agbalumos as you want. Everybody else gets only one.' Everyone looked on with envy as I picked five juicy agbalumos. I knew exactly what I was going to do with them.

Mrs Folawiyo asked all of us who had received an award to stand behind the cake so that she could take a picture. The giant cake was covered in orange icing with orange stars in a circle. In the middle it read 'Congratulations, Nile House'.

We shouted out 'Nile House' as we blew out the candles on the cake to a thunderous applause from everyone else.

When I walked back to my spot beside Caro, I bent down and gave all five agbalumos to her. She put both hands to her cheeks and opened her mouth with pleasure.

'What's this for?' she asked.

'For being better than agbalumo!' I grinned at her. She smiled her biggest smile and gave me one.

I pressed mine to make it soft but Caro bit into hers straight away.

The stars had started to come out.

I looked up at them and smiled at Caro. 'Turns out, I never had to write to you.'

'Because I was here all along,' Caro replied.

'Swear you'll always be there,' I said.

She put her forefinger on to her tongue and lifted it to the sky.

I did the same. We linked our pinky fingers together and laughed.

Our small group had now become quite large on the lawn with Tayo and Michelle joining us, along with Lola, Bukky, Flanky and a host of Senior Funmi's friends. Everyone was sucking on an agbalumo, relaxing, when Tope nudged Caro. 'Your dancing was on another level.' Ngozi jumped to her feet pulling Gemini with her. She began to chant and dance. Everyone got up and joined in.

All we are saying, dance one more dance!
All we are saying, dance one more dance!

ACKNOWLEDGEMENTS

To God, for the gift of writing.

To my parents, for starting a good story.

To every person I went to boarding school with, you are the story.

To every person who ever loved my stories, you cheered me on.

To Golden Egg Academy, for helping me pour it on the page.

To Emma Greenwood, for taking it further.

To Rachel Leyshon, efiko editor.

To Chicken House publishers, you took it to the finish line.